"What are you nervous about?"

If her face got any hotter, her blood was going to steam right out of her ears. "Nothing, and good night, Mr Forrest. You should go play with your debutantes," JD said as she turned to go.

His hand on her shoulder stopped her dead in her tracks. "I'm not interested in any debutantes."

She sent up a breathless prayer for her fleeing common sense to get back where it belonged. But the light touch of his fingers on her shoulder didn't move away, nor did her common sense trot on back to the barn. "Mr Forrest – "

"Most of the crew calls me Jake." His fingers finally moved, sliding down her shoulder, grazing over her bare elbow beneath the short-sleeved shirt, only coming to a stop when they reached her wrist. He pressed his thumb against her frantic pulse. "But not you, not even after all these years. Why is that?"

"I like to keep things professional." Unfortunately, her low, husky voice sounded anything but.

Available in September 2010
from Mills & Boon®
Special Moments™

A WEAVER BABY

BY
ALLISON LEIGH

MILLS & BOON®

All the characters in this book have no existence outside the imagination of
the author, and have no relation whatsoever to anyone bearing the same name
or names. They are not even distantly inspired by any individual known or
unknown to the author, and all the incidents are pure invention.

First published in Great Britain 2010
Harlequin Mills & Boon Limited,
Eton House, 18-24 Paradise Road, Richmond, Surrey TW9 1SR

© Allison Lee Johnson 2009

ISBN: 978 0 263 87998 8

23-0910

Harlequin Mills & Boon policy is to use papers that are natural, renewable
and recyclable products and made from wood grown in sustainable forests.
The logging and manufacturing processes conform to the legal environmental
regulations of the country of origin.

Printed and bound in Spain
by Litografia Rosés S.A., Barcelona

Allison Leigh started early by writing a Halloween play that her school class performed. Since then, though her tastes have changed, her love for reading has not. And her writing appetite simply grows more voracious by the day.

She has been a finalist for the RITA® Award and the Holt Medallion. But the true highlights of her day as a writer are when she receives word from a reader that they laughed, cried or lost a night of sleep while reading one of her books.

Born in Southern California, Allison has lived in several different cities in four different states. She has been, at one time or another, a beautician, a computer programmer and a secretary. She has recently begun writing full time after spending nearly a decade as an administrative assistant for a busy neighbourhood church. She currently makes her home in Arizona with her family. She loves to hear from her readers, who can write to her at PO Box 40772, Mesa, AZ 85274-0772, USA.

Prologue

"Heads up." The warning came in accented English. "He's got her highness with him."

J. D. Clay gave Miguel a wry smile. "She can't be that bad." The man who owned the thoroughbreds she and Miguel Perez worked with *had* married the "highness" after all. Jake and Tiffany Forrest even had twin sons, though in the short time since Miguel had hired J.D. to work in the stables at Forrest's Crossing, she hadn't yet seen the boys.

"She's worse," Miguel said under his breath as he put a wide smile on his face while the couple in question strode along the hectic shed row toward them. "Beautiful an' no good for da boss."

J.D. frowned a little, but she'd quickly learned that gossip and rumor were always ripe in the stables, particularly when it came to Jake and his beauty-queen wife. They looked like they belonged on a movie screen rather than here, with dirt under their feet and the perfume of horse manure in the air.

Tiffany Forrest was ivory skinned and black haired. A modern-day version of Snow White, only this one had an elaborate race-day hat perched on her head that would have cost the dwarfs their entire mine. And her tall, athletically built husband, Jake, was simply the description in the dictionary beneath TallDarkandHandsome. Together, the two were—well, *striking* didn't even come close.

They stopped next to the stalls that had very tasteful bronze *FC* plaques on them, and J.D. watched the man's brown, intensely sharp gaze rove over his thoroughbreds there. One, Metal Cross, was running in the Kentucky Derby later that afternoon. His stable mate, June Cross, had won the Kentucky Oaks—a race for fillies only—the day before. "Everything set to go, Miguel?"

"Sí, sí." Miguel was head trainer for Forrest's Crossing and the diminutive Peruvian grinned widely. "Metal here, he gonna do it for us this year. Bring you the roses jus' like when your daddy won 'em."

"That's what I want to hear." Jake's coffee-brown eyes skipped over Miguel's head. "J.D.," he greeted. "Everything looking good with our filly, there?"

Before J.D. could offer a response, the glossy woman at his side looked up at him with a smile that was only exceeded in brilliance by the jewels draped almost nonchalantly around her throat. "Jake, everyone's waiting for us up top," she reminded.

"We've got time," Jake assured. He was still looking at them and missed the sexy pout his wife aimed his way.

J.D. didn't. "Junie's in great shape, Mr. Forrest," she said as she ducked under June's neck and moved to the far side, running the soft brush over the beautiful filly's flank. She didn't need to see the superior glint in Mrs. Forrest's eyes to confirm that she was much more suitable inside the stable, than outside of it. "Metal's going to run just as great as Junie did, yesterday."

Jake's smile was slightly crooked as he tucked his hand around his wife's rail-thin waist and turned to go. "Then we'll see you in the winner's circle, won't we?"

"Oh, Jake." J.D. could hear Tiffany laughing lightly as she walked away with her husband. "Don't go getting that poor girl's hopes up. *She's* not going to be there with us."

J.D. kept grooming June. She already knew that if Metal ran his way to the winner's circle, it would only be the owners, their trainer and the jockey smiling for pictures and accepting trophies and winnings. She'd be back here, mucking out the stalls and polishing up tack.

She was part of the stable woodwork while the couple was definitely Millionaire's Row.

They were welcome to it.

Give J.D. horses any day of the week. They never disappointed her. And *she* never disappointed them.

Chapter One

Five years later

"You didn't go out with the rest of the boys?" Jake's voice was deep and in some fanciful part of J.D.'s mind, she imagined it felt like a soft blanket sliding down her bare skin.

"I didn't want to cramp their style." She sent him a smile over her shoulder, but the wryness of it was mostly for herself. As the only female in the entire stable crew at Forrest's Crossing, she'd never been one of "the boys." She was simply an assistant horse trainer on Jake's sizable payroll who—according to Miguel—usually had one too many opinions of her own.

Though this time, her opinion when it came to Latitude had proved right on the money.

Literally.

From the first burst out of the starting gate to the way

the thoroughbred sailed across the finish line of The Sanford, the horse had been pure poetry in motion. He'd raced as brilliantly as J.D. had known he could, so of all the crew from Forrest's Crossing, she was probably the least surprised.

And except for Latitude Crossing's owner, Jake—who'd collected the tidy first-place purse he didn't remotely need—she was probably the happiest.

Satisfaction curved her lips all over again, and it didn't even matter that Miguel had been the one to claim the glory of Latitude's unlikely win. He'd been so elated, he'd told the stable crew that drinks were on him, and they'd all tumbled out of the barn, looking ready to continue the celebration that had been going on since they'd touched down in Georgia from Saratoga.

Even though it was late, J.D. was still celebrating, too; but she preferred to do it in the company of the *real* winner.

She folded her arms over the top rail of the stall, looking at the gleaming bay contentedly munching his way through fresh feed as if he had done nothing remarkable at all. "Look at you acting all modest," she chided the colt. "You ought to be wearing a crown."

"The Triple Crown," Jake murmured behind her.

That shiver dashed down her spine again. She'd like to blame it on the prospect of Latitude joining those few elite horses in history that had attained the coveted achievement, but she'd never been one to lie to herself.

The shiver came from Jake. Not from the idea of Latitude finding the elusive Triple Crown glory in the coming year.

"His chance at that is nearly a year away," she said. The famous races that comprised the Triple Crown were run by three-year-old thoroughbreds only, beginning in May with the Kentucky Derby, the Preakness Stakes two weeks later and capped off with the Belmont Stakes in early June.

Which meant a thoroughbred had one chance in their lifetime to accomplish the feat. "And who knows what Miguel
will want to do between now and then," she added practically. Miguel fired people at the drop of a hat. The fact that
she'd survived his mercurial nature for five years was a
record for Forrest's Crossing.

"If he's smart, he'll leave you alone with Latitude. Miguel's
more interested in Platinum Cross, anyway." Platinum was
sired by one of Forrest's Crossing's most successful horses.
But even Metal Cross hadn't brought home the "crown." He'd
won both the Preakness and the Belmont. But he hadn't won
the Derby. Nor had any other horse for Jake.

They still made the trek every year to Churchill Downs.
The only things that changed were the names of the thoroughbreds running for him, and the names of the glossy women
on his arm who'd revolved through his world since his divorce
shortly after J.D. came to Forrest's Crossing.

He folded his arms over the top rail next to her, holding an
open bottle of Cristal in one hand and a slender champagne
flute in the other.

He held them just as casually as if they were a dime-store
mug and a long-neck beer. But the expensive champagne was
much more in keeping with the off-white silk shirt he wore.
And the crystal flute was probably of the irreplaceable, antique
variety, inherited from his father and great-grandfather just as
he'd inherited Forrest's Crossing.

It wasn't the quality of the champagne or the stemware that
made her nerves jumpy, though. There was wealth in her up-
bringing, too. Just not on the scale of Jake's.

His family owned Forco, one of the largest textile firms in
the country. For him, thoroughbreds were merely a personal
passion that he could well afford to indulge. And where his
family was into jets and setting, *hers* was more into jeans and
settling down.

No, what made her nerves want to dance a jig had one, simple cause.

Him.

She slid her gaze away from his arms and those long, lean fingers, focusing again on the oblivious colt as she discreetly tried to put a little space between their arms. She needed every inch she could get just to breathe around the man.

"Miguel will take over again now that he's seen for himself what kind of heart Latitude has," she predicted, clinging to the thread with a desperation that she prayed didn't show. Miguel was the head trainer. J.D., an underling. He had every right to make whatever decisions he wanted.

"Does that bother you?" Jake shifted slightly and his arm grazed hers, right across that spare inch she'd managed to gain.

She sucked in a silent breath and made herself remain still. It was no easy task. "Crossing the finish line first isn't what I love about horses." Her voice was blithe.

Latitude lifted his head, his large, liquid eyes looking into hers. He blew out a noisy breath, as if he were laughing at her nonchalance.

She stared back into the colt's eyes. *Mind your own business, Lat.*

He snorted again and stretched his long neck over the rail, butting his nose against her shoulder.

She fell back a step, laughing softly despite herself.

Jake steadied her and he nudged Latitude's head away. "Behave."

"He just wants this." J.D. pulled a peppermint out of the pocket of her FC-emblazoned polo shirt. She unwrapped the mint and held it out.

Latitude eagerly nipped the candy off her palm.

"Can't blame him for that." The corner of Jake's mouth curled slightly and his gaze seemed to linger on her shirt.

More specifically, on the pocket above her breast.

Admittedly, it had been years since she'd even flirted with a man, but she wasn't so out of practice that she didn't recognize interest when it—all six-plus feet topped with thick brown hair and hooded eyes—was staring her in the face.

Her cheeks heated when her nipples pinpointed eagerly beneath the butter-yellow cotton.

She stepped back to the rail, careful to keep that space between her arm and Jake's. Squashing her breasts against the hard rail didn't do a thing, though, to squash the warmth zipping around in her veins.

If she'd had such an infernally predictable response to Donovan, maybe they wouldn't have broken up six years ago. But then again, she knew they would have. Donny hadn't liked coming in second to her beloved horses. And he'd especially not liked coming in second to another man—Troy.

She'd learned her lesson, though.

Stick to horses and nobody gets hurt.

She could feel her face getting hotter by the second and avoided Jake's gaze. Having the hots for the owner of the horses she loved was *so* not high on her list of how to succeed in what was commonly perceived as a man's world.

She'd always been fine before with her particular affliction where Jake was concerned. Because she was just a lowly soul on his stable crew. One he barely looked twice at, much less looked at the way he was looking now.

"Something wrong? You're looking very…flushed."

She wanted to bury herself in a pile of straw. "I'm still not used to the humidity here," she defended with a shrug that even *she* didn't buy.

"It's just a warm Southern night." His voice was like molasses. Vaguely amused. Darkly sweet.

She had another peppermint tucked in her breast pocket and wondered if it could melt because of the heat steaming through her. "With about a gazillion percent humidity."

He tipped the champagne bottle over the flute and shimmering, golden liquid bubbled forth. Then he held the glass toward her. "Maybe this will help you cool off."

She couldn't help laughing. "I think I've already had too much of that." The first bottle of bubbly had been opened at the track in New York. And it had been followed by several more on the flight in his personal jet that made the trips to New York and Florida and California easier on the horses.

"Yeah, but you didn't have Cristal," Jake drawled. "Live it up, J.D. It's just one night."

She knew she should decline. But she still closed her fingers around the smooth, delicate crystal, brushing against his warm fingers as she did so.

Her heart skittered around. She couldn't manage to look away from his face. "I'm not exactly a champagne kind of girl." And not at all *his* kind of girl.

"What kind of girl are you?"

The kind who was getting out of her depth fast, and should be old enough to know better. Her fingers tightened around the glass. "Strong coffee when it's cold and a cold beer when it's not."

A faint smile hovered around his lips. "Not that I'm knocking either one, but this is a special occasion. Latitude's won his first race. One of many, if all goes well." He tucked his finger beneath the base of the glass and urged it upward. "Live it up. You might like it."

There were a lot of things she was afraid she would like, more than was good for her.

Champagne was at the bottom of that list.

Jake Forrest was at the top.

All of which did not explain why she still lifted the glass to her lips and inhaled the crisp aroma as she slowly took a sip. And once she did, she couldn't help the humming sigh of appreciation that escaped.

The fine web of crow's-feet that arrowed out from his eyes crinkled even more appealingly. "I knew you'd like it."

How could she not? It was like swallowing moonbeams.

Then he lifted the flute out of her fingers and put his lips right where hers had been.

He might as well have touched her with a live wire. But judging by the flare of his pupils as his gaze stayed locked on hers, he was perfectly aware of that fact.

She swallowed, hard, and stepped away from the rail again. Some temptations were wiser left untouched. Jake might be divorced, but that didn't mean he was available.

So, she swept her hands down her jeans to hide the fact that they were shaking and kept her shoulders square. "It's getting late. I'd better—"

"Are you afraid of me, J.D.?"

Her jaw loosened a little. Fear would be easier to deal with. "Of course not."

"Then why are you ready to bolt?"

She opened her mouth to protest that, but how could she? She *was* ready to bolt.

And yet, when he lifted the crystal glass and grazed the cool rim ever so faintly against her lower lip, she seemed frozen in place.

His voice dropped another notch. "What are you nervous about?"

If her face got any hotter, her blood was going to steam right out of her ears. "Nothing." She snatched the glass from him and inelegantly chugged the remainder, then pushed the glass back at him. When he didn't take it, she reached past his broad shoulder and balanced it on the corner post of Latitude's stall. "Good night, Mr. Forrest. You should go play with your debutantes." She turned to go.

His hand on her shoulder stopped her dead in her tracks. "I'm not interested in any debutantes."

She sent up a breathless prayer for her fleeing common sense to get back where it belonged. But the light touch of his fingers on her shoulder didn't move away, nor did her common sense trot on back to the barn. "Mr. Forrest—"

"Most of the crew calls me Jake." His fingers finally moved, sliding down her shoulder, grazing over her bare elbow beneath the short-sleeved shirt, only coming to a stop when they reached her wrist. He pressed his thumb against her frantic pulse. "But not you, not even after all these years. Why is that?"

"I like to keep things professional." Unfortunately, her low, husky voice sounded anything but.

"You're the epitome of professionalism."

She couldn't help it. She looked up at him through her lashes. "Pardon me, but I don't feel that way just now."

His coffee-brown eyes would have looked sleepy if not for the heat blazing from them. "Your job is secure no matter what. Miguel is in charge of the stable crew."

"And you're in charge of Miguel."

"Miguel is in charge of Miguel," he corrected wryly. He upended the rest of the champagne into the flute and lifted the glass again. "But if you insist on going, take this with you, at least. You, more than anyone, has earned some very fine champagne today."

"Latitude did all the work."

"Latitude ran for *you.* Miguel wanted me to sell him until you started handling him."

Jake wasn't telling her anything she didn't already know. She took the glass. Felt her head swim as she sipped again at moonbeams.

And somehow she found the toes of her scuffed boots boldly brushing the toes of Jake's highly polished ones. She wasn't even sure if his arm came around her waist first, or if it was her hand pressing against the solid warmth of his chest.

But the crystal flute was suddenly caught between them, the glittering liquid spilling as their mouths found one another.

Champagne moonbeams were no comparison at all when it came to the taste of Jake Forrest.

It made her weak. Deliciously weak.

And there was no earthly way she could convince herself that one kiss would be enough.

Not when his splayed fingers were hard and hot against her spine through the thin knit of her shirt. Not when his other hand slid along her shoulder, cupped her cheek, fingers threading through her hair, urging her head back. Not when she felt the murmur of her name in his low, deep voice whispering along her neck before he pressed his lips against the pulse at the base of her throat.

Her mind reeled, trying to find reason. Or justification. Jake was a worldly man. He wouldn't expect anything later that she wasn't capable of giving.

Her fingers flexed against him, encountering champagne-damp silk and cool crystal. Then the glass fell, landing with a soft shatter when Jake lifted her off her feet until her mouth was level with his again. "Do you still want to run?"

She could feel his heart thudding hard against her. Her fingers clutched his broad shoulders. Their faces were so close, she could have counted every one of the dark, spiky eyelashes that surrounded his gleaming gaze. "Do you *want* me to run?"

He pressed her against the paneled wall next to Latitude's stall and ran his hands along her thighs, drawing them up, alongside his hips. "What do you think?"

Every unyielding inch of him from shoulder on south pressed into her and she had to choke back a moan. "Mr. Forr—"

His mouth cut her off. "Jake," he said against her.

Her hands slid behind his neck. His thick hair was cool between her fingers. "Jake," she obliged breathlessly. She'd have said anything as long as he didn't take away the intense pleasure of his kiss. "Jake," she said again on a low moan of delight when his weight pressed even harder into her. Her fingers slid from his hair to curl into the smooth silk covering his back, pulling it up until she could feel the warmth of his satin-smooth flesh instead.

A deep sound rumbled from him to her and she couldn't just hear his want…she could taste it. Then his hands clasped her rear and she was vaguely aware of glass crunching beneath his boots as he carried her into an empty stall, and she almost cried out at the loss when he settled her on her unsteady feet.

But the loss was mercifully brief. He knelt before her, dragging the hem of her shirt from her blue jeans, shoving it up as his mouth pressed, open and hot, against her abdomen. She swayed, clasping his shoulders, only to draw his hands greedily to her breasts when they hovered so close, so teasingly near.

His thumbs dragged the thin cups of her lacy bra aside, raking tauntingly over her tight nipples and needles of delight shot through her. She yanked off the strangle-hold of her twisted shirt and slid bonelessly to her knees. She felt blind to everything but the fire burning in Jake's eyes; couldn't look away from him as his long fingers slid away from her breasts to meet at the zipper of her jeans. "Don't stop now," she whispered.

A muscle flexed in his angled jaw and he pulled down the zipper. Before she could shimmy out of the jeans, though, he tipped her back and she felt the scrape of soft, fresh straw against her spine.

"Boots." His voice was a low, husky drawl that was as arousing as his touch. He pulled off her boots and tossed them aside.

Her impatient hands reached out for him again then, but he pushed to his feet, and she could only lie there, breathless with tightening desire, as he pulled off his own boots. The silk shirt followed as he yanked it over his head, not even bothering with the buttons.

Then his hands fell to the belt at his waist. Her mouth ran dry as he slowly pulled it loose, dropping it aside, right along with every other stitch he wore.

She wasn't exactly a virgin. She'd had two lovers before, brief though those failed relationships had been. But it was still good that she was already sprawled in the straw because the sight of all that male glory made her dizzy. Dark hair swirled across his muscular chest, narrowing to a fine line over his tight abs, just inviting her to follow its trail.

And then he was pulling at her jeans, sliding them off her hips. His lips pressed against her navel, and the heat inside her threatened to explode as she nearly bowed off the ground.

"What happened here?" His fingers smoothed over the faint remains of a long-healed scar that peeked above the edge of her pink panties.

"Stepped on by a horse."

He trailed the line up and down. "Must've hurt."

Agonizing in ways she didn't let herself think about anymore. "You work around horses, you're going to have some bruises somewhere along the way."

His lips kicked up. "First time I fell off, I was five."

"Six." She shifted, impatient for him to get beyond the cotton panties. And he seemed to realize it because his mouth traced the thin scar as he drew the hank of fabric down her thighs with an intensity that made her feel perfectly beautiful and unscarred.

His breath whispered against her abdomen. "Are you sure?"

She couldn't help the strangled laugh that quivered up her throat. Her thighs shifted restlessly and she reached for him. "I'm dying here," she managed.

"Impatient." The edge of his white teeth flashed for just a moment as he slowly moved over her. "I like that."

She wanted to sink her teeth into his shoulder when he didn't move fast enough to suit her, and she pushed at him, flattening him on his back with a speed that had those crow's-feet crinkling again. "I am impatient," she whispered. "I haven't done this in a long while." In one smooth arch, she took him in.

Her breath stopped. Her heart stopped.

The world might have stopped, too, except she was too busy staring into the unholy pleasure that tightened Jake's face to notice. He sucked in a sharp breath and closed his hands hard and tight around her hips. "How long a while?"

She shook her head. How could she care about details that didn't even merit comparison to *this?* "It doesn't matter. Years." She slowly worked her hips against his, and knew with feminine instinct that it felt as torturously perfect for him as it did for her.

He sucked in another hard breath. "You're dangerous."

"Next time, think twice before you give me Cristal."

She felt his bark of laughter down to the very center of her, and then neither one of them was laughing as he rolled her in the straw and sank even deeper. "You feel incredible," he breathed against her ear.

What she felt was a climax bearing down on her with the speed of a freight train. Her head twisted in the soft straw. "Jake—"

"Forget the warm summer night." He pushed up on his forearms, tendons tight in his neck. His shoulders. "*You're* a storm."

And she felt suddenly buffeted. She cried out, the cataclysm spiraling even harder because Jake was right there with her, his own satisfaction flooding through her.

It seemed endless, that pure pleasure that streaked through her veins, heating her from fingertips to soul. And maybe it was endless, because by the time Jake finally drew in a deep, shuddering breath and rolled over on his back, his arms splayed in the straw, J.D. knew the world could have come to a halt and she wouldn't have noticed.

She let out a long, shaking breath of her own. She couldn't have moved just then to save her soul.

"Wow," he murmured after a while.

She almost giggled. And she'd never much been a giggling sort. "I think I'm still vibrating."

He huffed out a faint laugh. "Honey, flattering as that is—" his voice was a low, sexy drawl "—I think that might be my cell phone." He pushed himself up until he was sitting, his intoxicating gaze roving over her as he tugged the edge of his trousers out from beneath her hip. He pulled out his vibrating cell phone, his gaze meeting hers with a devilish humor. "Never going to be able to talk on this thing again without thinking about…today."

She wanted to roll over and bury her hot face in the straw, but his hand settled on her bare flank. It was vaguely appalling that she felt a stirring all over again, even when her entire body drifted in satiated stupor.

But then his phone vibrated again and he checked the display. The humor in his face died and he drew back his hand.

Despite the hot night, J.D. felt a sudden chill.

Then he hit a button and set the phone to his ear. "Tiffany. What have the boys done now?"

Chapter Two

"Thanks for agreeing to meet me."

Jake rose from his chair and eyed J.D. where she stood, just inside the door of his study. "Of course." He waved at the leather chairs situated in front of his desk. "Have a seat."

Her green eyes didn't meet his as she crossed the room. But instead of sitting, she stopped behind the chair closest to the opened French doors. She closed her fingers over the back of it and her knuckles were white.

He bit back a sigh.

Since that night in the barn more than a month ago, they'd only seen one another a handful of times. For minutes only, when it came right down to it. But even then, the brief encounters had felt awkward.

Not because he regretted touching her.

But because it was so clear that *she* did.

"You didn't tell Mabel why you wanted to meet with me." His personal secretary had been quite put out as a result. But

Jake could have told Mabel that he already had a good idea why J.D. had requested a meeting. It was something she'd never done before in all the time she'd worked at Forrest's Crossing. If there was an issue at the stable, she would have gone to Miguel.

Which, to Jake, meant only one thing.

She was going to quit.

"I thought it best not to tell Mabel the specifics." J.D.'s fingers whitened even more over the back of the chair. "Actually, I tried to get an appointment with you at your office at Forco, but your secretary there was even less accommodating than Mabel. She said you had nothing available on your calendar there until November."

"Lucia is my assistant, actually. And she controls my schedule at the plant more than I do." He wanted to go around to her and peel those fingers away from the leather, urge her down into the seat and tell her anything that would make her relax.

He remained where he was. Things would be better all around if he refrained from touching her, since he already knew he seemed unable to exercise much control where she was concerned. Touching her was flammable. They'd already proven that. "You could have just phoned me directly, you know. Avoided the others altogether."

Her face looked a little pinched. "I don't have your direct number."

He frowned a little at that and immediately pulled out a business card. He scribbled on the back of it. "Now you do." He handed it to her. "Would you like a drink? I can call Mabel—"

"No." She took the card gingerly. "No, thank you." She glanced over her shoulder as if she were afraid that his secretary would already be standing behind her.

But the door to his office was firmly closed.

They had all the privacy either one of them could want.

He dragged his mind out of that dangerous direction.

"How are things down in the stable?"

Her slender throat worked. "They're not too happy, needless to say. Everyone had high expectations for the Hopeful last week. I'm sure you did, too."

Despite the thrilling success at Latitude's maiden race, followed up by an even more spectacular finish at the Saratoga Special, Latitude had fallen far short at the Hopeful Stakes, coming in damn close to last. "Yes, I did. My sisters and I expect winners, not losers." That's what Forrest's Crossing did— produced world-class, winning thoroughbreds. "And you?"

She lifted one shoulder and her yellow FC shirt tightened over the subtle, high swell of her breasts, needlessly reminding Jake of that night. "I'm never disappointed in Latitude."

Because she was the only one in his stable crew who wasn't motivated by winning, he knew.

"I think you'll have him more than ready for the Champagne Stakes," he assured.

If anything, J.D. looked even more strained. "The Champagne isn't until next month. But I didn't come to talk about Lat, actually."

Which just confirmed his fear that she *was* there to resign.

"Well, before you get started, I *do* want to talk about him." He took shameless advantage of still being the boss. "I'm telling Miguel that I don't want anyone but you working with Latitude. Not even him."

At that, her lashes flew up and those gut-wrenching green eyes of hers finally met his. Even the waves in her pale blond hair seemed to spring with shock. "If this is about what happened between us, then—"

"It isn't."

She very nearly snorted. She even released that whitened grip on the chair to lift her hands up in the air. "You've never made decisions around Miguel before. He'll have a fit."

"Miguel works for me," Jake reminded.

At that, she laughed out loud. "You yourself said nobody was in charge of Miguel. He *allows* you to keep him on the payroll because he chooses to be here. He could go anywhere in the world if he wanted and work with two dozen owners instead of just one. But he stays, and you let him run the stable the way he wants to run it because he brings you winners. And I know for certain that he wouldn't put me in charge of Latitude."

"Lat won his first two races because you were working with him. Miguel took over again before the Hopeful and he barely wanted to finish."

Her eyes widened and her bow-shaped lips pressed together. Evidence that she'd thought he was unaware of some details. "Just because I've been away on business for two weeks doesn't mean I don't know what's going on in my own stable," he said. "Miguel may not want to face the fact that you have the magic touch where Latitude is concerned, but I have, which is why I'm assigning you specifically to him. Miguel can focus all of his energy on bringing along Platinum. Of course, that means your fee will increase and—"

"Stop." She shook her head. "This is all wrong."

"You don't want to work with Latitude?"

She tossed up her hands. "Well, of *course* I want to work with Lat. I love that colt, but you need to know—" Her voice cracked to a stop. She looked away from him again. "You need to know that I'm, well, that I'm—"

"Excuse me, Jake?"

They both stared at the woman who'd had the audacity to open his closed office door. Only it wasn't his secretary, who would have known better. It was Jake's aunt Susan who rushed into the office.

"What's wrong?"

His aunt barely gave J.D. a glance as she hurried toward him, her slender hands twisting in front of her.

"Bill Franks just called me. Mabel put him through to me since you were busy." Her gaze flicked for a moment to J.D. "There's been an accident."

Everything stilled except Jake's guts. Bill and Jennifer Franks were his ex-wife's in-laws. "The boys?"

She hurriedly waved her hands. "No, no. Connor and Zachary are fine."

Relief slammed through him. His twin sons were fine. "Sidney? Charlotte?" They were his sisters, and aside from Susan who'd lived at Forrest's Crossing since he'd been a boy, the only other family who mattered to him.

Again his aunt shook her head. "It's Tiffany. She and her husband were driving—the boys weren't with them—they had an accident."

"I, um, I'll just excuse myself…." J.D. was edging toward the door, looking pale and even more awkward.

"Wait." He focused on his aunt's face. He generally didn't think about his ex-wife, except to curse her very existence. And to know that even *she* was a better parent than he was to their precocious twin sons. "How bad was it? Is Tiff hurt?"

"Her injuries are critical. Her husband—"

"You *can* say his name." They all knew it, after all, since the man had been in the picture long before Tiffany decided marriage to Jake was no longer her heart's desire.

Before Adam Franks had become Tiffany's lover, he'd been Jake's friend. His best man, in fact.

Susan hesitated, looking grave. "Adam's injuries were extremely severe. He didn't survive."

Jake slowly sat down in his chair as he absorbed that. There'd been plenty of times he'd cursed his one-time friend. But he'd never wished him dead. "Where are the boys?"

"With Bill and Jennifer still."

Adam's parents.

"Obviously they're not up to keeping them for any length of time," his aunt continued, looking worried. "But I just can't see sending Zach and Connor back to boarding school under these circumstances. They were very close to Adam."

Jake's gaze fell on J.D. She'd reached the door. "We can finish this later," she said softly. "You have more important things right now."

He grimaced and wanted to insist that she stay. He wanted her to stay at Forrest's Crossing. Period. And just acknowledging the thought was enough to remind him that he was the selfish bastard Tiffany had called him.

He'd barely given a short nod before J.D. slipped out the door.

It felt like she took all of the fresh air there was right along with her.

He looked back at Susan. "You talked with the boys?"

She nodded. "They're upset, naturally."

He didn't ask the next obvious question. There was no need.

If he'd been a better father, his boys would have wanted to speak to *him*.

He rubbed his hand down his face. "I'll have to go to California. You'll come, of course."

The boys were always more comfortable with her than they were with Jake.

"I can't." Susan's face was torn. "The gallery showing is Friday, and then I'm hosting the charity ball on Saturday in Charlotte's place since she had to go to that conference in Florence in *your* place."

He'd forgotten his aunt's photography showing. "Sidney can host the ball."

"Sidney is in Germany trying to buy that horse she's got her heart set on." Susan paced. His mother's sister was in her mid-50's, but there wasn't a gray hair to be found in her soft blond hair. The only real hint of her age was in the soft lines that had begun forming alongside her dark brown eyes.

"There are times when I wish y'all would just settle on textiles or on horses."

"Textiles help *pay* for the horses," he reminded needlessly. Raising and running thoroughbreds wasn't a poor man's game. It hadn't been for his grandfather or his father before him. "The boys'll have to make do with me."

"Oh, Jake. Don't talk that way. Naturally, the boys will want you."

She was trying to protect his feelings, as if he had some. But that was his aunt. The eternal optimist.

He, however, was about the exact opposite. He didn't have faith in the positive outcomes of life. He couldn't see the bright side of every situation.

He saw things exactly the way they were and when something needed doing, he did it. Right or wrong.

Bill and Jennifer were the only grandparent "figures" his sons possessed. Tiffany's parents had died when she and Jake were still married. Jake's father was dead, too. And he didn't know, or care, where his mother Olivia was, much less whether she was still alive. After she'd profitably washed her hands of them all, they'd never seen nor heard from her again.

Susan was twisting her hands together again. "I can join you after the charity ball is over."

He knew his aunt would turn cartwheels if it meant helping someone else. And he also knew he would take complete advantage of that fact, just like he always had.

Just like his father had before him.

Jake was exactly like his old man. They didn't just share the same name. They shared everything else. From looks to temperament to talents. Jacob Forrest, Sr., had been a selfish bastard, and Jake Forrest was carrying on the tradition in the best of old-South ways.

"Tell Mabel what's going on. I'll fly out this afternoon."

Susan looked relieved as she quickly left his study. Which

made him wonder if even his devoted aunt had doubted his ability to do the decent thing where his sons were concerned.

He pushed out of his chair, looking out the bay windows behind his desk. From his vantage point, he could see only the steeply pitched roof of the main barn well off in the distance.

His bedroom upstairs afforded a better view. Not only of the barn, but of the rest of the stables, and the training track.

He'd spent a lot of mornings standing at the window of his room waiting for a glimpse of J.D. to arrive.

She always appeared shortly after dawn, when the first glimmer of sunlight would catch her slender, leggy form that was so easily eclipsed by the massive horses she tended. Often, he'd see her riding Latitude, her long curls flying out behind her as she leaned low and close over the horse's back.

Even before Jake had gone to the barn that unforgettable night, those mornings spent watching J.D. even from afar had been the best part of his day. A slice of private and pure sanity in an otherwise insanely pressured life.

But now, unless he could talk her out of quitting, he was going to lose even those simple moments.

He shoved his hand through his hair and left by the French doors that opened to a spacious deck.

It would have been easier to drive one of the plentiful farm vehicles down to the stables. Instead, he walked across the acres of richly groomed lawn, taking the time to file away his feelings about the situation awaiting him in California.

It was the middle of the morning, and the track—when he reached it—was a beehive of activity.

He immediately spotted J.D. hosing down Latitude while Jake's wizened head trainer stood alongside her. Miguel stood a full head shorter than she did. Hell, the diminutive former jockey stood a head shorter than everyone.

Jake walked closer until they noticed him and the hose in J.D.'s hand jerked a little, though she said nothing.

"Jake," Miguel greeted him in his thickly accented voice. "I'm glad you come down today. I wan' you to sign off on some—"

"Actually, I need to speak with J.D.," he interrupted. If he let Miguel get his hooks in, it'd be hours before Jake would break free. And right now, that was time Jake couldn't afford. "Now."

Miguel's graying eyebrows pulled together in a fierce frown. He snatched the hose from J.D., his displeasure evident.

For that matter, J.D. didn't look any more enthusiastic, but she accompanied him into the sprawling building nearby that housed Miguel's office. He waited until she was inside the untidy room before closing the door.

She glanced from the door to his face. "I'd rather leave that open."

"I'm not going to jump you."

Her lips tightened. "I didn't think you would."

Problem was, he *was* always thinking about touching her. It had only gotten worse since he'd found out exactly how addicting that particular delight was. "I have to go to San Francisco," he said, corralling his thoughts. "Tiffany needs—"

"Of course," she cut in quickly. Dismay darkened her eyes from brilliant green to a soft moss. "I'm sorry to hear your wife—"

"*Ex*-wife."

Her head dipped a notch. "Well, I'm sorry about the accident. I'm sure your children will be relieved when you get there."

He doubted it. "I want your promise that you're not going to cut and run while I'm gone."

Sympathy drained away as she stared at him. "I beg your pardon?"

"The reason you wanted to meet with me was to turn in your resignation, wasn't it?"

Her silky lashes drooped, shielding that wide gaze. "And *that's* why you dangled Latitude in front of my nose?"

"I dangled Latitude because I want you training him to win. It has nothing to do with what happened between us."

A hint of pink bloomed over her cheeks. "And if I told you I hadn't been planning to give you my notice?"

He wouldn't believe her. There was no other reason to explain why she'd asked to meet with him. She never had before. And it wasn't as if she wanted a repeat of that night. She'd made that abundantly clear when she'd raced out of the stable that night, barely taking enough time to pull on her shirt and jeans.

"Lat runs best for you." He focused on the facts. "And I want to go to the Kentucky Derby next May knowing he's going to run his heart out for you. Bringing home a Derby winner's the only thing my father and grandfather succeeded in doing that I haven't."

J.D. looked pained. "That's just it. By May, I'll have other things I'll be focusing on."

"What? Like offers? Honey, I know you get job offers from other trainers every time we go to a meet. But I'm asking you not to decide anything yet. Wait until I get back from California, at least." He caught her slender shoulders, ducking his head to look into her face when she tried looking away. "Don't let what happened a few weeks ago make you leave Forrest's Crossing. I'll talk to Miguel about you taking over Latitude before I go."

"Six weeks ago." Her gaze flicked up to meet his, only to skitter away again. "This is not going at all how I intended."

She exhaled and looked weary as she pushed a racing schedule off the seat of a hard-backed chair and sat down. "Go to California, Jake. Your family needs you. We'll talk when you get back."

She hadn't agreed to stay beyond that, but for the moment, he'd take what he could get.

When he got back, there'd be plenty of time.

Chapter Three

The last thing J.D. expected to see were two brown-haired heads sticking up over the side of her pickup bed when she came out of the Chinese restaurant. The brown paper bag of take-out she held slid right out of her nerveless fingers, landing with a plop on the pavement next to her feet.

It was Friday evening at the end of a very long, miserable week; she'd just spent over an hour fighting rush-hour traffic into the city, and the only thing she'd been looking forward to was a meal that required no work, and then bed. Maybe not even in that order.

"Zach. Connor." Her voice was excruciatingly pleasant, as if she greeted Jake's twin sons in the back of *her* pickup truck every day of the week. "What are you doing?"

"Going for a ride," Zach replied with a "duh" sort of tone.

"That wasn't very bright of you when you had no way of knowing where I was going."

"You're going home," Zach returned just as quickly. "Arentcha?"

J.D.'s lips tightened a little. Jake had brought his sons back with him less than a week ago, and in that space of time, they'd managed to cause all manner of mischief around the place—from painting the legs of one of Miguel's favorite broodmares fluorescent pink, to parachuting out of their upstairs bedroom using bedsheets.

It was a testament to their true creativity that they hadn't managed to break their legs in that particular endeavor.

This, however, was the first time they'd directly involved J.D. in one of their stunts.

"Does it look like I live here?" She gestured at the busy little restaurant behind her where she'd just retrieved the food that was now sitting on the ground.

Connor frowned a little. "She's *not* home," he whispered to his brother. "And I gotta pee."

"You always gotta pee," Zach muttered. He sat up on his knees and folded his arms over the side of the truck, looking at J.D. with vivid curiosity. The hot, humid evening had caused messy tendrils of his brown hair to stick to his rosy cheeks. "I told Connor that you wouldn't know we was back here, and I was right."

A roadster waiting for her parking spot tooted its horn, and J.D. absently waved it on. "I have to call your father."

Zach rolled his eyes. "Jake won't care. He knows you'll take us back."

"Oh? Why are you so sure of that?"

"'Cause he said you always do what's right."

Her jaw tightened so much that it hurt. "Does he?" She wasn't entirely certain how Jake would have come to that conclusion. "Get out," she ordered, and watched while they scrambled out of the truck bed.

She felt like an idiot for not having noticed them back

there before now, and supposed it was a measure of her pre-
occupation that she hadn't.

The two boys came to a stop next to her.

Connor stooped to pick up the bag of food and peered
inside. "I bet they're fixing dinner by now." He held the bag
toward J.D. with a slightly more sheepish look on his face than
the one on his brother's. "You're lucky it didn't all spill out,"
he told her. "Are those egg rolls?"

She ignored his hopeful look and took the bag from him
before yanking open the truck door. "Yes. Get in."

She waited until the boys were inside, then set the bag on her
seat while she dragged out her cell phone and the business card
that he'd given her. But all she got was his voice mail. She left
a message, but then also dialed the house at Forrest's Crossing.

Despite the hour, it was Mabel who answered. "I'm sorry,
Ms. Clay," Mabel told her in the same stiff voice she'd used
two weeks earlier when J.D. had refused to tell the woman
exactly *why* she'd needed to meet with him, "but Mr. Forrest
isn't available for calls."

J.D. turned her back on the boys, only to turn around again
just as quickly to keep her eyes on them. For all she knew,
they'd decide to go joyriding in another person's vehicle. "He
hasn't left town again, has he?" She'd have heard so from
Toby, the new groom, who seemed to take great delight in following the activities of their wealthy boss.

"No, he's in town."

"Then this is a call he might want to take," she advised
flatly. "Regarding his sons."

"Perhaps you misunderstood. Mr. Forrest is not available."

Her hands tightened around the phone. "Mr. Forrest's sons
are with me in the city," she returned through her teeth. "They
were hiding in the back of my truck. Somehow, I think he's going
to want to know that, Mabel. Just in case he gets to wondering
where they are when they don't sit down at the dinner table!"

"Good heavens." The woman's tight voice softened a fraction. "But I'm afraid he really isn't here. He ran out to the plant a few hours ago."

J.D. pressed her fingertip to the pain that began throbbing between her eyebrows.

The two boys were sitting in the truck watching her with wide eyes and listening with wider ears. She pulled out the container of crispy, fat egg rolls and handed them to Connor, along with the napkins.

Then she turned away from the children and lowered her voice. "In that case, you'd better tell his aunt." *Someone* had to care where these boys were. "It's the middle of rush hour. It's going to take me more than an hour to drive them back home again."

"I'll be sure to tell her right away. The twins were really hiding in your car? This is going to upset Mr. Forrest," the woman fretted.

Considering it was the twins' first week at Forrest's Crossing, J.D. privately thought Jake might have been wise to forgo matters at Forco for a few more days. Forrest's Crossing might have been a little safer.

Instead, the very day he'd arrived with them, she knew he'd left town that night and hadn't returned until just a few days ago.

Even though she knew she should, she hadn't found a moment to speak with him privately again.

"I'm leaving the city right now," she said. Then caught the way Connor was wriggling in his seat. "Well, after a quick pit stop, anyway." She didn't wait for some response from Jake's personal secretary, but ended the call and tossed the phone onto the dashboard.

Then she waved the boys out of the truck. "Come on. You can hit the bathroom inside." She locked up the truck after them and followed them back into the busy restaurant, pointing the way to the restrooms down a narrow hallway.

They came out within minutes, craning their necks around as if to take in every inch of the busy, congested little restaurant. The hunger in Connor's expression was perfectly obvious, and she silently bid goodbye to the food waiting in the truck. "Did you wash your hands?"

Zach made a face. "We're not kindergartners."

That was plainly obvious. Even at nine years old, the Jake miniatures seemed tall for their age. "No kidding. Did you wash your hands?"

Connor snickered a little as he nodded.

Zach—obviously the more blasé of the two—just rolled his eyes before finally nodding.

She gestured toward the exit again. "Then let's go."

There were even more cars lined up in the full parking lot when they reached her truck again, and the moment the boys were buckled into their seatbelts and she pulled out of the spot, another car pulled in. "You might as well eat the rest." She gestured at the bag sitting in the console.

They didn't need any more urging and they practically tore apart the bag in their eagerness.

"When did you have lunch?"

Connor lifted a shoulder. He was wearing a red T-shirt and cargo shorts. Zach, busily unwrapping a plastic fork and spoon on the other side of him, wore blue jeans and a white T-shirt with some unreadable logo on the front.

"We didn't," Connor said. He didn't wait for a plastic utensil, but picked out a piece of sweet-n-sour pork with his fingers and popped it in his mouth before handing off the container to his brother and fishing in the bag for another.

They were gulping at the food so fast she regretted not stopping long enough to buy them something to drink. As it was, she didn't even have her usual bottled water with her. And her air-conditioning was barely keeping up with the heat billowing up from the nearly grid-locked interstate. "Do you always call your dad *Jake?*"

Connor looked inside the paper bag as if he were hoping that more containers would magically appear inside of it. "Adam is our dad."

Zach jabbed his fork into the sweet-n-sour pork. *"Was,"* he muttered.

Which had J.D.'s heart squeezing.

Was it any wonder they were now finding some mischief? "I heard about what happened," she said quietly. "I'm very sorry."

Connor's head ducked, focusing harder on the rice.

"No big deal," Zach said.

J.D. gave them a glance before turning her attention back to the traffic crowding it's way along the interstate. Both boys were focusing intently on their food.

"I think it would feel like a very big deal to me," she told them.

"That's 'cause you're a girl." Zach looked out the side window. "Guys don't get all upset like girls do."

"Ah." She tucked her tongue between her teeth.

"Can I turn on the radio?" Connor asked. He was clearly ready to change the subject.

"Sure."

He leaned forward and fiddled with the dials and buttons and within minutes, he and Zach were squabbling over what station to listen to. J.D. just let them go at it.

They might be boys, but as far as she could tell, they didn't sound a whole lot different than she and her sister Angeline had sounded when they'd been kids.

She and Angel had argued together just as much as they'd laughed together. And when J.D. had landed in Georgia, Angeline had soon followed. Only instead of mucking out stalls and hot-walking blood horses, her sister had become a paramedic. They'd rented a small house together in a quaint old neighborhood and that's where J.D. had stayed after her sister moved back to Wyoming and became Mrs. Brody Paine.

She sighed faintly. She still missed Angel.

Now, more than ever.

The pain between her eyebrows deepened.

The sun was nearly set by the time she pulled up in the stately drive outside the mansion.

Jake's lethal-looking sports car was parked in front of the marble steps and J.D. didn't have to wonder if he'd received her voice mail or been informed of the boys' activities, because he was standing on one of the steps. Obviously waiting.

J.D. pulled to a stop behind his car and gave the boys a sideways glance. "Judging by your dad's expression, I'd say he cares quite a lot about what you've been up to."

Even from the distance and the dwindling light, they could see the dark expression on Jake's face.

And the twins looked as if they'd just as soon spend eternity sitting in her cab to getting out and facing the music.

She had a small bit of sympathy for them on that score. She was none too anxious to face Jake right now, herself. And given that, the smile she sent into the boys' disgruntled faces was a little less sharp than it might have been. "Out you go."

"He looks kinda mad," Connor said.

Zach huffed and snapped off his seatbelt. "What's he gonna do? Send us back home to boarding school? He's already said that's what he's gonna do." He shoved open the door and slid out onto the ground, all bravado and cockiness.

Connor followed a little more slowly. "Thanks for the food."

Bemused, she could only nod.

She could have put the truck into gear and driven away, but instead, she hovered there long enough to see the boys trudge up the shallow, wide steps toward their father. She could see them speaking, but couldn't hear the words.

A moment later, the boys were stomping through the ornate

front door and J.D. was wishing that she'd resisted her lingering hesitation and just driven away, because once Jake's focus was off his sons, it turned like a laser toward her.

Something sharp jangled through her.

She swallowed around the constriction in her throat and rolled down the window when he came down beside her truck.

He ducked his head so he could see through the window and she could see the rough shadow forming on his angular jaw and smell that faint, lingering scent of him that her memory had been hanging on to with fiendish delight.

"You're not really sending them home to boarding school, are you?" she blurted.

His brows drew together. "Excuse me?"

The words were out there, so she couldn't very well take them back even if she wished she could. At the very least, though, she might have phrased the question more tactfully. "Zach mentioned you planned to send them back home to school."

"And you clearly disapprove."

The growing heat in her face owed nothing to the hot day. "I'm sorry. It's really none of my business."

Before she could stop him, he'd pulled open her door. "I don't know. They chose *your* truck to stow away in. Maybe that makes it your business. So yeah. Mabel's already made the arrangements. They'll be back terrorizing the halls of Penley next week."

Knowing it wasn't her business wasn't enough to keep her from protesting. "But, Jake, they're still upset about the accident. They should be with family. If you're worried about them missing school, enroll them here. Or hire a tutor or something!"

"They'll be better off at Penley than here with me. And they'll be able to visit their mother if they're back at school. Tiff's housekeeper will cart them back and forth."

She tried to imagine it and failed.

And Jake obviously read her expression all too accurately. "Tiffany's the one who enrolled them. She wants them near her, now," he said. "And there's nothing wrong with a boarding school. I went."

"Did you like it even when you weren't grieving?"

The arrow seemed to find its mark and his face tightened. "At least they won't be pulling more stunts like this."

"They're upset and acting out."

"They always act out," he returned. "Upset or not."

"Don't you wonder *why* that is?"

"Yeah." He looked annoyed. "And when you have kids of your own, maybe we'll sit down and solve all the mysteries that come with them."

She swallowed. Hard. What *did* she know about raising a child? Her nerves jangled and she brushed her hands down her dusty jeans. "I'm sorry. And I'm sorry that I didn't realize they were in the back of my truck right away. I don't know why I didn't." Yes, she did. She was too busy thinking about her own particular problem than to notice anything else. She flushed even hotter under his steady gaze.

"And I'm sorry they inconvenienced you. Come in the house."

"No, really." She tried to pull the door shut again. "I should be getting home."

"Plans?"

Her lips flapped uselessly. She couldn't seem to come up with a lie to save her soul. "Not…really."

His gaze went past her to the spent Chinese-food containers. "Connor said they ate your dinner. The least I can do is feed you in return." He reached right in and pulled her keys from the ignition and took her elbow. He tugged her inexorably out of the cab and weak-willed woman that she was, she went.

But when her boots clomped on the marble steps, she held back again. "I smell like stable." The last—and only time—she'd been inside the mansion had been two weeks ago. And she'd made darn sure she hadn't smelled like horse sweat and manure first. She wasn't a beauty-queen type by any stretch. But even *she* had her pride.

Then she wished she'd just kept her mouth shut, because Jake lowered his head until she could practically feel his soft inhalation.

"Smell okay to me," he murmured. His gaze—much too close—caught hers. "So, what's the problem?"

She swallowed hard and carefully took a step away from him. "No problem. No problem at all."

Of course that was one big, fat lie considering she was nearly eight weeks pregnant.

With *his* child.

Chapter Four

Eating dinner in the mansion wasn't anything like J.D. had expected it to be.

They were seated in the formal dining room around a linen-draped table that could have sat a football team, but there was nothing formal about the meal.

Jake had a stack of papers next to his plate and seemed content to split his attention between them and J.D.

Of his sons' actions that afternoon, he was evidently not planning to make any more comment. At least not in front of her.

Zach and Connor sat at the table, too, but since her Chinese food had taken the edge off their appetites, they paid more attention to the electronic hand-held games they were playing than they did to the meal. And that was set on the table by Jake's aunt.

Her legs felt unsteady and she sank down into her chair again looking from Jake to his boys and back again.

Would he show as little interest in their child as he seemed to show for his twins? Would he have his secretary *make ar-rangements* to pack her off to boarding school when she in-evitably got up to mischief? Would he practically ignore her every time they sat down together for a meal?

The thoughts made J.D. a little dizzy and she quickly reached for the crystal water goblet, inelegantly sucking down half of its contents.

Of all things, *that* Jake seemed to notice. "Are you all right? You look pale."

Heat streamed through her cheeks, right on up to the tips of her ears. "Fine. It's just been a long day."

His lips twisted. "That it has been."

Her gaze flicked to the boys. Neither one looked up from their hand-held games, despite the plate of food their aunt set in front of them.

Susan took the seat next to J.D.

"Put your papers aside, Jake. What sort of example are you setting?" Her gaze went to the boys. They'd stopped playing their games in favor of pulling ghastly faces at each other.

"Zach, Con, put the games away," he said. Though he didn't set aside his papers at all, J.D. noticed. She also noticed just how tired and drawn he really looked. It seemed plain that the past few weeks had taken a toll on him.

Then Jake's gaze encountered hers and try though she might, she couldn't quite make herself look away.

Susan's intentionally cheerful attempts at conversation with the boys faded into the background.

J.D.'s field of vision seemed to narrow and pinpoint on the quizzical lift of Jake's eyebrow.

Even the air seemed to thicken until her lungs struggled for oxygen.

"Whoa." Jake suddenly bolted from his chair, catching her before she slid sideways off her chair.

"Dude," she heard one of the boys—probably Connor—breathe.

"Take it easy." Jake's voice came close to her ear and she frowned, focusing with an effort.

Her head was swimming. "What?"

"You looked about ready to faint," Jake said.

His hands were on her shoulders, she realized. She could feel the press of his fingertips through her T-shirt and much too easily she remembered that night.

The night they'd conceived a baby that she'd believed she'd never have.

Her stomach clutched. "I'm sorry."

"Here." Susan was nudging a water goblet toward them. "Give her some water."

Jake lifted the glass to J.D.'s lips and it was just easier to succumb than to fight. She sipped at the water, and gradually, the room seemed to straighten.

The line between his brows had deepened even more. This close, she could see his eyes were bloodshot.

How long had it been since he'd slept?

She straightened in her chair, pressing her shaking hands along the sides of the upholstered seat. "I'm fine."

"We can all see that." Jake didn't smile.

"Here you go, dear." Susan had managed to fill a plate with food and she set it in front of J.D. "A little food and you'll be good as new."

There was nothing unappetizing about the juicy pot roast and roasted vegetables, but J.D.'s stomach lurched horribly anyway. "Actually, if I could just freshen up for a moment?" Still feeling dizzy around the edges, nausea forced her rapidly to her feet and she practically ran out of the room when Susan pointed out the directions.

J.D. barely made it to the fancy powder room near the marble foyer before she lost her lunch.

After, she rinsed her mouth and sat on the closed commode with the sink faucet still running, and pressed her face into her hands.

Since the moment that the big blue plus sign had appeared on the home pregnancy test she'd taken, she'd felt myriad things. But this was the first time she'd felt the slightest hint of morning sickness.

It made her pregnancy seem a little more real. She didn't know whether that made her want to laugh or cry.

"J.D.?" The concern in Susan's voice was evident even through the closed door. "Do you need anything?"

J.D. dropped her hands and looked at her reflection in the mirror opposite her. A husband?

"No." She cleared her throat, and looked away from the mirror. Becoming pregnant had thrown her for a loop, a joyous one certainly, but that didn't mean she was entertaining ideas about orange blossoms and I do's.

She was 31 years old and more than ready to be a mother. But a wife?

She hadn't been able to stay faithful to Donny and he was the closest she'd ever come to even considering marriage.

"No, thank you," she finished more clearly, and turned off the water before opening the door. "I'm fine," she insisted. "It's the heat. It's just getting to me more than usual today."

Susan's eyes, so like her nephew's, weren't convinced, but it was probably her good manners that kept her from arguing the point. "It is awfully hot," she agreed, and fell in step with J.D. as they headed back to the dining room. "I'd like to think the boys were simply miserable hiding in the back of your pickup truck the way they did," she confided softly. "It might make them think twice next time before pulling another stunt."

"Did'ja throw up?" Zach asked the second she entered the dining room.

"Zach," Jake admonished.

The boy hunched his shoulders and jabbed his fork back into the slice of pie on his plate. "What? I was just curious."

"Maybe you got the flu," Connor suggested. "I got it last year. I got to miss a whole week of school 'cause of it. It was cool even if I did gotta throw up. Do you get to miss work now?"

"I don't have the flu," J.D. said. "I certainly don't have to miss work."

"Maybe you should," Jake suggested. "Miguel told me there was a bug going around down there. Maybe you've caught it."

The bug she had wasn't exactly catching.

But it did provide an excuse and she greedily latched onto it. "Maybe so. Which means I should go before I spread it to all of you."

"Jake, she shouldn't drive," Susan protested.

"No, really—"

"My aunt is right." Jake set down his pen and stood. "I'll drive you home."

"No!" She seemed to be saying that quite a lot now, when she ought to have said it that night in the stable, eight weeks ago. "Truly," she tried in a more reasonable tone, "it's not necessary. I'll be fine." She started backing out of the room again. "I, um, I even have the entire weekend to rest up. Stay here with your family. Enjoy your meal." Though, with the exception of Sophie, it didn't look like anyone was enjoying themselves much. "Thanks." She gave a little wave and turned on her boot heel, hurrying back toward the foyer.

Rude or not, she wanted—needed—to get out of there.

The stress inside the Forrest mansion was absolutely palpable and while she felt some sympathy for Jake's boys, she wasn't in any position to change anything.

She had a pretty good-sized situation of her own to resolve already.

She made it all the way to the front door and out to the wide front step before Jake caught up to her. "Hold it."

Feeling like a disobedient schoolgirl did nothing to improve her sense of awkwardness.

She forced her tight shoulders down where they belonged and looked back at him, lifting one eyebrow.

She worked for him, and yes, she'd been unthinkingly careless to have unprotected sex with him, but that didn't mean she was his to order around. Not when she wasn't on his time clock. "Excuse me?"

His tired face tightened. "Wait, J.D., please," he amended. "I'll drive you home. You're in no condition—"

She quickly went down the shallow steps. "I said I'm *fine!*"

Again, he caught up to her, this time taking hold of her arm to stop her flight.

Her pulse stuttered as she looked from his hand to his face.

A muscle flexed in his jaw and his hand slowly fell away. "Do you dislike me that much now that you can't accept a simple offer?"

Shock swept through her. Dislike wasn't at all what she felt when he touched her. "I don't dislike you."

His hands spread slightly. "Well, honey, it's definitely feeling that way."

She raked her hand over her hair, and yanked out the band around her ponytail when her fingers tangled in it. Her hair fell loose and heavy past her shoulders. "Jake, it's just not a good idea. Okay?"

"Why? Because you're afraid that people might—" he ducked his head toward her and lowered his voice "—*talk?*"

"Go ahead and make fun. You're up here in your ivory mansion." She jerked her chin toward the copse of trees that led down to the stables. "I'm down there with a half dozen guys who gossip worse than any quilting circle they have back home." She came from Weaver, Wyoming, a small town with its own highly developed grapevine. She knew gossip, and the guys she spent most of her time with were some of the worst.

"All I need is for someone to catch a glimpse of me riding around in that car of yours, and I'll be suffering through their trying to get me to trip up where you're concerned."

"What are you talking about?"

"Miguel believes you assigned Lat exclusively to me because I exercised my feminine wiles over you!"

"I told him—"

She huffed out a breath. "It doesn't matter what you told him. It doesn't matter what you say. They judge based on what they see and what much more interesting story their minds can create. They're a group who believes in the theory of where there's smoke, there's fire." And heaven knew there'd been plenty of fire between Jake and J.D. that night.

When she wasn't trying to figure out what was the best thing to do now, she was still feeling scorched by the memory of those flames.

"I'll get Miguel straightened out."

She couldn't help but laugh a little, though there wasn't much humor in it. "The more you try to fix the situation with Miguel, the more he's going to think what he already thinks." Her hands lifted to her sides. "And the fact of the matter is, he's right. You assigned Lat to me because…because—"

"I thought we'd gotten that straightened out."

"All we did was put off the matter while you dealt with your wife's accident."

"I told you before. *Ex*-wife," he corrected.

Her gaze snuck to the mansion behind him. The gracious dwelling had never possessed a replacement for her—the only woman he'd ever cared enough about to marry. "It doesn't matter anyway." She drew her thoughts away from that direction back to where they belonged. Everything that went on in the tight, surprisingly small world of thoroughbred racing had to do with reputation. All Miguel had to do was voice one hint that J.D.'s "promotion" where Latitude was concerned occurred because of her personal relationship with Jake, and she'd never be judged on her real merit again. She'd never be taken seriously as a trainer once she left Forrest's Crossing.

That would be true even if there were only rumors.

Jake's gaze sharpened even more. "If it doesn't matter, why are you making an issue about it?"

No matter what Jake's reaction would be when he learned about the baby, she knew she couldn't continue to work for him. And thanks to the gossip about them, she wouldn't be able to work anywhere else. Not in the blood horse world, anyway.

She hadn't gone to him before to resign, though he'd thought so at the time. It was almost ironic, really. Even without knowing she was pregnant with his child, he'd seen that reality before she had.

"I can't work here anymore, Jake," she said. "I'm sorry." And she really was.

"I don't want you to go."

Something inside her clutched—hard. Her hands went sweaty and she swallowed. "Why?"

His jaw flexed. "Latitude runs for you, J.D., and you know how much I want to be in the winner's circle at the Derby next May."

She prided herself on having her eyes open where Jake was concerned. So the pang she felt was considerably sharper than it should have been. "Latitude runs because he loves it. But Miguel will have Platinum ready for the Kentucky Derby, too. He has just as good a chance as Latitude. And the Derby is still eight months away, anyway. Tell Miguel to put his nephew Pedro on his back for the Champagne Stakes. I've seen the kid on the track and with Latitude. He'll do fine. And if Miguel isn't the right handler, you'll find someone else who is."

"I already *did,*" he said pointedly.

The back of her throat felt tight and achy. On any other day, she might have felt like she *was* coming down with the bug that was going around the place. For Jake, everything revolved around him winning. And it was the height of irony that it was the colt she so loved that was now making it more impossible than ever. "I can't stay, Jake."

"Because of what I did to you."

She closed her eyes for a moment, pained. "What *we* did." Honesty wouldn't allow her to let him shoulder that. "For heaven's sake, Jake, I was more than willing, in case you've forgotten."

He shoved his hands through his hair, then scrubbed his palms down his face. "Willing or not, I should've known better." He dropped his hands, but the grimace was still there. "You're the kind of woman who probably thinks you're supposed to want to marry a man when you're sleeping with him. Or at least be in love with him."

She folded her arms across her chest. "Don't be ridiculous."

He lifted an eyebrow. "You're saying that you're not old-fashioned when it comes to sex? You, who hadn't *done this* in a long while?"

She flushed. Trust the man to remember what she'd said to him that night. "Being discriminating doesn't necessarily mean a person is old-fashioned."

"Then why the hell *can't* you work here, anymore?"

Tell him.

The command circled inside her head. Her lips parted; the words sitting on the tip of her tongue, ready to trip off.

That ache returned to the back of her throat. She'd seen him with his sons. She looked up at Jake. "Because I'm going home," she finally said.

His brows drew together. "Home. What the hell's that supposed to mean?"

Her eyes stung and she looked back at her practical, dusty

Chapter Five

J.D. swallowed the knot of nervousness inside her when she pulled up at the big house, which was how most people referred to the main house at the Double-C ranch where her father and his four brothers had grown up. There were already a dozen cars parked on the circular gravel drive, meaning there were twice that many people *inside*.

She'd been back in Wyoming for two weeks now, and aside from the first weekend when everyone had descended on her parents' place to welcome her home, she'd been busy enough looking at properties to buy to avoid too many family get-togethers.

But today was her niece's birthday and there was no way she could get out of making an appearance.

She wove her way through the haphazard congestion, parking almost at the back of the house, right on the grass.

It hadn't snowed yet that year, but signs of the dropping October temperatures were visible all around, most notably on the grass that was turning brown and crisp. She climbed out of her truck, her eyes roving over the wide-open expanse of land surrounding the outbuildings. For as far as the eye could see—and beyond—the land was owned by one member of the Clay family or another. They ran cattle, raised dairy and bred horses.

And she, she would be boarding horses, just as soon as she could get the run-down property she'd bought that week for a song into decent enough shape. She didn't mind the work ahead of her.

It would leave her with little time to think about everything—and everyone—she'd left behind in Georgia.

"You gonna stand out here and daydream, or go inside?" The slightly rough voice brought her attention around to the tall man leaning against the house, a thin trail of smoke winding upward from the cigarette he held.

The sight of her cousin, Ryan, was still enough to jar her.

For one thing, he'd gone missing years earlier. And after years of searching and years of hoping, they'd accepted the worst. They'd grieved. They'd had a funeral for him. Then, earlier that year, he'd miraculously shown up on the night of their cousin Axel's wedding. For another thing, the smiling, wry Ryan with whom she'd grown up was nowhere in evidence within the utterly solemn, grim man who'd returned. He was only five years older than she was, but could have passed for ten.

They'd all wept for joy, anyway. He was still Ryan. He was still one of their own. And the fact that he hadn't explained his absence to a single member of the family was his business. And frankly, something she sort of understood a little better these days.

"Cigarettes will kill you, you know," she told him, instead of answering.

"Something ought to." His lips barely twisted as he lifted his hand to his mouth to inhale.

She rounded her truck, heading to the stairs that led to the rear entrance of the big house. "Guess we're all hoping that doesn't come any sooner than we'd already believed." Before he could comment, she snatched the cigarette from between his fingers and ground it beneath her heel. "Nobody around here wants second-hand smoke, either."

His blue eyes narrowed. "Still bossy, J.D.?"

She patted his unshaven cheek. "Come inside."

He grimaced. "You know, there are twenty teenage girls in there."

"Surely *you're* not afraid?"

"Hell, yeah." He practically shuddered.

She tucked her arm in his and tugged him toward the stairs. "Be brave." She winked at him as if she'd had no reservations of her own about showing up there. "There'll be cake and ice cream afterward if you're good."

He exhaled, but went up the stairs with her, pulling open the wooden screen door for her. She felt Ryan's faint hesitation as they entered the kitchen, which was crowded with people—mostly the preteens Ryan had expected. He'd been back for a solid seven months, but it was plainly obvious that he had to make an effort to be among crowds—whether formed by family or not.

"Hello, sweeties." Their aunt Jaimie noticed them first. "Work your way through. Ryan, your dad is playing bartender in the basement well away from these young ladies if either of you are interested in something other than cider and lemonade." She smiled humorously. "Your uncles are down there hogging the pool table as usual."

"Grandma," Megan, the birthday girl, wrapped her arms around Jaimie's waist, "*please* can I take my friends out to see the kittens before we have lunch? Grandpa already said we could, as long as we didn't climb in the barn rafters." She giggled. "Like we're crazy enough to do that."

J.D. laughed. More than once, she'd heard the story about Jaimie doing just that while trying to rescue a cat—a cat Matthew still maintained hadn't needed rescuing at all. "Yes, who would be crazy enough to do that?"

Jaimie shooed her away with a wave as she dropped a kiss on her adopted granddaughter's nose. "You may go to the barn. But we'll be ready to eat in a half hour so be back by then."

Ryan headed straight for the basement stairs as the chattering girls moved en masse toward the back door. J.D. quickly shifted out of their way before she got caught in their wave. "Where's Mom?"

"Aunt Maggie's in the dining room with Mom," Megan called out before she scampered out of the kitchen on the heels of the departing.

Jaimie blew out a breath when the screen door swung shut with a bang after them. "Every year I suggest having Megan's and Eli's birthday parties out here, and every year once the hoards descend, I wonder if I've lost my mind. Sarah and Max might not have as much room as we do, but they certainly have more energy!"

"You love it," J.D. reminded, and her aunt's dimple flashed as she turned back to the trays she was filling with food. J.D. left her and headed to the dining room to find her mother and her cousin arranging cups and plates on the table. "Need help?"

Maggie gave J.D. a quick kiss and Sarah shook her head, making her strawberry-blond ponytail sway. "We're almost finished in here. For sanity's sake we're doing buffet style."

Maggie lifted her chin toward the doorway that led out to the family room. "Your brother is here already. Said to tell you to hurry because that horse race is about to start. It's on in the basement, too. Everyone wants to see that horse of yours."

J.D. managed a smile. "He's not my horse." Since there was nothing for her to help with, she headed into the family room where most of the furniture was already occupied. She should have known that nobody in the family would forget that the Champagne Stakes was being run that afternoon. The Champagne was a prestigious race for two-year-olds.

She almost wished they would have.

She'd spent most of the day picking up her cell phone to call Jake to wish them luck, only to set it down again without dialing.

She barely found a perch on a corner next to Tara—Axel's new wife—who was rocking their sleeping baby boy, Aidan. J.D. smiled at her and peeked beneath the edge of the blanket covering part of his cherubic face, but she turned quickly toward the large television when the horses burst out of the starting gate.

Her heart leapt into her throat and she sat forward, her eyes glued to the image of Latitude's powerful surge through the field.

"Looks poky to me." Her grandfather, Squire Clay, sat nearest the television, leaning even closer as he rested his hands atop the sturdy walking stick braced on the floor in front of him. "Platinum Cross is the favorite to win. He's already got the lead."

J.D. shook her head. "Platinum is a great horse, but Latitude'll come up by the final turn. You watch."

Someone turned the volume up, and the room seemed filled with the pulse-pounding hooves.

"Eighth in the first turn. You know that jockey?" J.D.'s father, Daniel, moved behind her. His hand covered her shoulder and squeezed.

"Pedro Perez. He's Miguel's nephew."

"Well, he's got your horse in a helluva lot of traffic," Squire sniffed. "They need some room."

And they weren't finding it. She clasped her hands together and blew into her fists. *Come on, Lat. Run just because you love it.*

Squire slapped his knee as Latitude suddenly found space and surged to the outside where J.D. knew he liked to run best. "Look at that boy move!" He shot J.D. a grin. "Our girl taught him that."

She smiled wryly and shook her head. "That's all Latitude," she assured, still watching the television. The handsome devil's nose reached out, his black tail streaming out behind his powerful, mahogany body as he thundered forward, steadily overtaking one after another, until he was solidly in third. The commentator's words were as rapid as the hoof beats and as excited as the cheering from the stands as another horse, Sideofhoney, nosed ahead of Platinum who fell even farther behind. The field barreled toward the final turn and in the last seconds, Latitude surged in the backstretch, closing three full lengths to take the lead from Sideofhoney like it was a cakewalk.

"Hot damn!" Squire thumped his walking stick on the floor. "That is one fine piece of horseflesh." His pale blue eyes were sharp and clear as he looked back at J.D. "Winning that thing gets him a spot in the Breeder's Cup, doesn't it?"

"The Juvenile," she confirmed. Jake would be *very* happy. The Breeder's Cup was like the Super Bowl of horseracing. It drew the best horses in the world and was the richest weekend in the sport. And yet, J.D. knew that if it came to a choice for Jake, a win at the Kentucky Derby mattered more to him.

The television panned from the finish line to the stands where Miguel stood with Jake and his sister, Sidney, and his aunt. They were clearly elated.

There was no sign of Jake's sons with them.

Tucking her disappointment out of sight was more difficult than she expected, and she turned away from the television.

Zach and Connor's absence wasn't necessarily proof that Jake had sent them back to their California school, but it seemed likely. They might be able to visit their recovering mother more easily, but J.D. still felt bad for all of them.

Including Jake.

She murmured some excuse about helping in the kitchen, but knew that nobody was really paying any attention. Not when there was the usual amount of chaotic bantering going on. But she hadn't made it down the hallway before her father called her name.

She glanced back and something in his expression made her pause. "What?"

He held out his hand toward her. "Sideofhoney collided with Latitude. They both went down."

Everything inside her went abruptly numb. She pushed past him to stand in front of the television.

The sportscaster was on the screen, his perfectly coiffed hair and shining white teeth at odds with the silent video playing behind his shoulder of Pedro waving his hands to the crowd after the finish line, when the other horse suddenly pitched forward, veering into his path. Latitude stumbled and young Pedro jumped off his back, scrambling around to calm the abruptly frantic horses while people from all sides raced onto the track.

Horror surged through her as the bit of film was played again. And again. But the toothy sportscaster didn't give any more details other than the unconfirmed speculation that both colts had suffered injuries. After which he seemed to take grim delight in recounting the number of thoroughbreds who'd sustained catastrophic injuries while racing. "I have to call."

"Okay." Her father's hands pushed her toward a chair. "But sit down first. You're swaying on your feet."

Was she? She sat, simply because it took too much concentration to fight him. But then she realized she didn't have her cell phone. She'd left it in her truck. "I need a phone."

Word of the horses' injuries had obviously spread as the family room filled with even more of her relatives. All looking from her to the television and back again.

"Here." J.D.'s mother Maggie tucked a cordless phone into her hand.

J.D. focused hard on the keypad, shakily dialing first Jake's number from memory, then the number for the stable. Nobody answered there, either. Not even young Toby. She finally disconnected the call.

Already, the sportscaster had moved on to another story. It made J.D. want to throw her shoe at the screen.

A clattering from the kitchen announced the return of the birthday revelers, and she scrubbed her hand over her face. "I'm going to go home. I want to keep trying to reach them and I can't do that here. I don't want anything ruining Megan's birthday party."

"She'd understand," Sarah said.

J.D. knew that was probably true. Before her cousin and Max had adopted Megan, she'd already endured more in her young life than anyone should when her natural parents had been brutally killed. "You only get one thirteenth birthday," she said.

Maggie covered J.D.'s hands and rubbed them. "What can we do?"

"Pray."

It was Ryan who drove J.D. to her new home from the Double-C.

He didn't want to talk any more than she did. Nor did he try to coddle her with reassurances that when she learned more details about Latitude, it would probably be to learn that he was going to be okay.

For that alone, she was grateful, and didn't mind that his offer was probably more of an excuse to escape the birthday party than anything else.

Once inside her house, she sidled between moving boxes and turned on her television and her laptop computer. The Internet would probably have details more quickly about Latitude than the television. But the Champagne Stakes wasn't the media darling that some races were, and the sketchy details she *did* find were grim. Sideofhoney had been humanely euthanized at the racetrack. Latitude's condition was still unknown and by that night, she knew little more than she'd known at the Double-C.

She turned down the volume on the television and picked up the phone again.

She was so used to not receiving an answer, that when the ringing was abruptly replaced by Jake's rough-sounding, voice, she very nearly dropped the telephone.

"If this is another reporter, *no comment*."

"Jake, wait. It's J.D." She had to push the words past her tight throat. "Are you all right?"

He was silent for a moment. "Don't you mean is Latitude all right?"

Her throat constricted even more. She sank weakly onto the hand-me-down chair she'd pillaged from her parents' basement. "I mean all of you. Including Latitude."

"None of us is good. Including Latitude."

Which didn't tell her yet if the beloved colt was even still alive. She looked at the glassy darkness of the big picture window that had taken hours of polishing and her eyes stung. "I was watching the race," she finally said huskily. "You put Pedro on."

"And he won it for us." His voice was even. "Nobody expected Side to go down like he did. Jockeys with five times the experience as Pedro wouldn't have been able to prevent Lat's fall." He was silent for a moment. "He fractured his left rear cannon."

She tucked her tongue between her teeth. The cannon bone was akin to a human's shin. A break there was an almost guarantee against racing again. And if Latitude couldn't race…

"What are his chances?"

Again, Jake was silent for a painfully long moment. "Poor. Randy Windsor has his case."

"He's good." She knew the man's reputation. He was one

of the best equine surgeons in the world. The fact that Jake already had him on Latitude's case spoke both to Jake's influence and the severity of Latitude's injury.

She paced down the hallway to the kitchen that was just as crowded with moving boxes as the rest of the modest two-story was. "Has he already done the surgery?"

"Tomorrow afternoon."

"In New York?"

"Why do you care? Are you going to be here to see whether Lat even makes it out of the anesthesia?"

She jerked, feeling like he'd dealt her a physical blow. "Jake—"

He blew out a noisy sigh. "Yes. He's here. Miguel's with him."

"Where are you?"

"In the air."

She blinked a little at that. Going where?

She wanted to ask, but was afraid of the answer. If Latitude had no chance of returning to racing, Jake would probably be wagering the likely profits of rehabilitating the animal for stud purposes. Lat had only a few winning races to his credit, even though they were significant, graded races. And while he had a perfectly decent pedigree, it wasn't as stellar as some.

Which was why Miguel hadn't believed he would be a great racehorse in the first place. He believed that came from blood more than heart.

She closed her eyes and pinched the bridge of her nose. If she hadn't talked them all into giving Latitude a chance, the colt would be injury-free right now, romping around for some rich little southern girl's pleasure-riding delight instead of awaiting surgery for an injury that could be too severe—or too costly—to repair.

She dropped her hand and tried to keep her voice calm. It was nearly impossible. "Does anyone know what sent Side-ofhoney down like that?"

"Bobby Davis called me." He named the other colt's owner. "Said that Side broke both front ankles."

J.D. felt sick. "That poor thing. His rider?"

"He crushed a couple ribs and broke his wrist. He'll recover." A jockey's life was beset with injuries. "The racing stewards are reviewing it, deciding whether or not he should have pulled up Side during the race." A jockey could be fined, disqualified, or even barred from racing altogether, based on the officials' findings.

It was a horrible situation for anyone to be in. From the owner to the jockey. Not to mention the horse.

"Will you have someone let me know how the surgery goes?"

"I'll call you as soon as they contact me."

"You're not planning to be there." She turned away from the packing boxes and paced back into the living room. "Off to somewhere more important than Latitude," her voice was acidic.

"Actually, yes. The boys were suspended from school." His Southern-smooth voice was flat. "I got the call from the headmaster about the same time I was helping load Latitude into the ambulance."

Fresh dismay swamped. "I'm sorry. Why were they suspended?"

He was silent for a moment and in her mind's eye she could see him raking his long fingers through his hair. "They broke into the science lab in the middle of the night last night, and set off some sort of goo-bomb."

"Goo?"

"Sticky, slimy green stuff. The explosion spewed it all over the lab."

The vivid image filled her mind. "Was anybody hurt?"

"Just the lab mice's dignity. The little criminals weren't found out until the security cameras they'd rerouted to some Internet cartoon channel were fixed."

Given the circumstances, the huff of laughter that tumbled

out of her was thoroughly inappropriate. "I know I shouldn't laugh. But they're only nine. How'd they think up such things?"

"It's either laugh or cry," Jake said. "Take your pick."

She'd done both that evening. "Do you have a plan?" Foolish question. Jake Forrest *always* had a plan.

"Besides tar and feathers? Mabel's got a list of alternate schools for me."

Naturally. "Isn't it possible that the boys would prefer to go back to Georgia with you and that's why they pulled such a stunt in the first place?"

"No."

She bit her tongue, squelching further argument. Trying to understand Jake's behavior when it came to his sons only meant she'd end up second-guessing herself even more.

"I know one thing," he said after a moment. "Lat would be a lot calmer with you around. I could have a charter there to pick you up in a matter of hours. You could see Latitude before he goes into surgery. You could be there if he comes out."

If. The tiny word seemed to echo hauntingly.

"And then what?" Her voice went huskier. "I can't stay with him, Jake. Not for the kind of time his recovery is going to take."

"Then after Windsor finishes with him, he'll be in Miguel's hands."

"Miguel is an excellent horseman."

"Yes, he is," he agreed immediately.

She also knew that Miguel had never really bonded with Latitude. Not the way she had.

"If I go, and I'm not saying I will," she said, without really being aware that she'd begun contemplating it, "I'll take care of my own transportation." Making her own arrangements meant she'd be in control. She could leave when she decided.

"You'll go."

His confidence was as annoying as it was intoxicating. "*If*

I do, it doesn't change anything beyond seeing him through the surgery. You understand that?"

"I understand what you're saying," he assured smoothly.

Which, of course, did not mean that he *understood* at all. How could he, when he didn't know she was pregnant?

She was so intent on her thoughts that the knock that came on her door startled her. Her gaze went to the old-fashioned clock on the fireplace mantel.

"I need to go. Someone's at my door."

"It's nearly ten o'clock there. You have a lot of visitors this late?"

Did he actually sound jealous? "No, which is why I need to see who's there." She headed to the door.

"And what about Latitude?"

"I'll let you know."

"When?"

Her hand tightened around the phone. "When I decide," she said evenly. "Good night, Jake."

"J.D.—"

Her thumb hovered over the end button but she put the phone back to her ear. "Yes?"

"It was good to hear your voice."

Her heart squeezed, but there was nothing she could say in response, because as soon as he said it, *he* hung up.

The knocking on her front door sounded again, more insistently, and she flipped the lock and pulled it open.

Her sister, Angeline, stood outside, her long dark hair gleaming beneath the porch light. "I drove up as soon as I heard."

J.D. sucked in a breath and burst into tears.

Chapter Six

Angeline made a soft sound and stepped inside, wrapping her arms around J.D. and nudged the door closed behind them. She guided J.D. to the couch and held her until the awful racking slowed.

Her eyes felt swollen and her throat felt raw, but J.D. finally sat back, wiping her cheeks with her sleeve. "I don't know why I'm crying. I never cry."

"It's been a tough day for you."

J.D. laughed miserably. That was one way of putting it. "Where're your men?"

Angel smiled slightly and shrugged out of her coat. "Brody and the boy wonder are at Mom and Dad's. I told Brody I was fine to drive up myself, but he wouldn't hear of it. He'll have to go back to Sheridan tomorrow night, though. He's got a case in court Monday morning." She squeezed J.D.'s hand. "Early and I can stay if you need, though."

"You were here barely two weeks ago. Brody's going to

start getting annoyed with me for taking his wife away from him every time he turns around."

"I wouldn't worry too much about that if I were you." Angel's smile was serene. "I have ways of pacifying my husband."

J.D. pressed her hands against her closed eyes. "Latitude's scheduled for surgery tomorrow."

"That doesn't leave us much time to get there."

She dropped her hands to eye her sister. "Us? *I* haven't even decided to go."

"Of course you'll go."

"That's pretty much what Jake said." She pushed herself off the couch and went to the window, but all she saw was her own reflection. "As if he knows me so well."

Angeline joined her.

They were the same height, but any similarity ended there. J.D. was lanky and had Maggie's blond hair—only with an annoying curl in it—and Angeline was curvaceous with the exotic coloring and features of the Central American parents who'd perished when she was little more than a toddler. And though they'd both grown up as Clays, neither was one by birth.

After marrying J.D.'s mother, Daniel had adopted J.D., then both Maggie and Daniel had adopted Angeline. And from the moment J.D. and Angeline had met, they'd been like two halves of a whole.

Angeline was the one person who knew all of J.D.'s secrets. Good and bad. Yet J.D. still hadn't admitted to her what had happened between her and Jake.

"Everyone who knows you knows how much you love that horse," Angel pointed out now. "It's not such a leap. So what bugs you about it?" She pressed her dark head against J.D.'s. "Or is it just *Jake* in general that bothers you?"

"He doesn't bother me."

"He's always bothered you," Angel corrected wryly. "From

the first time you met him. Or have you forgotten that you and I used to live together out there?"

Of course she hadn't. "It's different now."

"Are you finally going to tell me why?"

J.D. looked away from their reflections. "It's not important," she lied.

"Oh, right. Whatever happened between the two of you sent you running here to Weaver. I'd say that makes it important."

"Who said anything happened?" She paced across the room.

"Bluffing at the poker table is one thing you can do. Bluffing with me is one thing you can't." Angel's gaze followed her. "You're pregnant, aren't you?"

J.D. stopped dead still. "What?" She looked down at herself. She kept waiting to see some significant difference in her body, but hadn't. She looked back at her sister, but denying it seemed fruitless. "How can you *tell?* Does anyone else know?" The idea that her family might have figured it out, but said nothing, was far more unnerving than her own reasons for delaying in telling them.

It wasn't as if they'd be angry with her. The Clays, to a one, were a deeply loving family. Not for a moment did she worry that she wouldn't have their love and support. The arrival of a baby in the family would be celebrated, unquestionably. But J.D. just wasn't ready to talk about Jake. Knowing her family the way she did, they probably weren't going to be too fond of her choice not to inform him of her pregnancy, no matter what her reasoning.

"If they do, they haven't said anything to me," Angel assured. "I thought you looked a little different when I came up after you arrived, but I couldn't put my finger on it. And now, you look even more so." Her hand swept down the front of her form-fitting ivory sweater. "Or maybe I can just tell because like recognizes like."

J.D. stared. "*You're* pregnant?"

Angeline smiled. "The doctor confirmed it just yesterday afternoon. About seven weeks along. You?"

J.D. sank weakly down on the couch. "Ten." She looked up at her sister. "I didn't think it was even possible to *get* pregnant."

"Because you have only one ovary left." It wasn't a question.

"And a fallopian tube full of scarring," J.D. added. "I went through all this with Rebecca when I was seventeen years old." Her aunt was a physician and ran the small hospital in Weaver. She'd attended to J.D. when her frantic horse had stepped on her as well as the snake that had spooked her.

"And as I recall, Rebecca didn't tell you it would be impossible for you to get pregnant, but that it could present difficulties in the future when you were ready to start a family. Difficult. Not impossible. Obviously," she added pointedly. "It's Jake's?"

"He doesn't know," J.D. admitted, hating the guilt that colored her voice.

"Is that why you're afraid to see him if you go to Latitude now?"

"Jake won't be there," J.D. said surely and told her about Jake's sons' latest act of mischief. "He thinks he has to stick them away in another boarding school again before he can get back to Latitude."

"So, he's seeing to his sons' needs before his own," Angel reasoned. "What about that has you angry?"

"I'm not angry."

Angel just watched her.

"Okay." She scrubbed her hands down her face again. "Maybe I am. But how Jake raises his children—" or doesn't "—has nothing to do with me."

"Right. You're just pregnant with one of his children and evidently making major decisions about it without consulting him." She lifted her hands peaceably. "Don't glare at me. I'm on your side. But if you're so convinced he's not going to be in New York, there's no earthly reason why we can't go there right now so you can see Latitude."

"I'm a big girl, Angel. You don't have to go with me."

"I know I don't. But I'm going, anyway. Early can stay with Mom. She's always begging me to bring him more often. If Latitude's surgery goes well, we'll celebrate with milk shakes and if it doesn't…" She tilted her head, her expression full of sympathy.

J.D.'s eyes filled again. "I've missed you."

"I've missed you, too." Then Angel dusted her hands together and cleared her throat. "So. You pack and I'll call the airlines. Deal?"

"Deal."

They arrived in New York with enough time for J.D to see Latitude before he limped into surgery with his leg wrapped in an immense compression boot. Though his head had come up when he saw her, the confusion in his eyes when they led him away had been heartbreaking.

And then it was time to wait. Wait as the minutes ticked into hours and the hours had through the entire afternoon. Miguel was there, periodically. He was polite when J.D. introduced her sister but it was plain that he considered their presence unnecessary. It was also plain that he considered the surgery itself to be a waste of effort.

"Jake should've let the track vet put him down when he attended to Sideofhoney," he said more than once. "Even Missus Sidney argued with Jake. It'll be a miracle if Latitude races again."

J.D. wanted to shout at the man that miracles *did* happen. And the miracle that counted right now wasn't whether Latitude raced again, but that he survived at all. Instead, she'd just turned away and walked to the other side of the waiting area.

About four hours after they arrived, they heard footsteps

again. But instead of the white-jacketed Dr. Windsor that appeared, it was Jake, looking every inch the wealthy businessman that he was in his perfectly tailored gray suit and silver tie.

She went hot, then cold, and was vaguely aware of Angeline's sideways glance as her sister finally stepped toward the man, her hand outstretched. "Mr. Forrest," she introduced. "I'm Angeline Paine. J.D.'s sister. I'm sorry we didn't meet before, under better circumstances."

"Jake, please." He shook Angel's hand, though his gaze strayed to J.D. "I'm glad J.D. hasn't been here alone."

J.D. folded her arms across her chest, mostly to stop the shivers that raced through her.

She hadn't seen him face-to-face in two weeks. She certainly hadn't anticipated the emotions swirling through her and she sorely wished she'd worn something more presentable than the black track suit she'd traveled most of the night in. "I thought you weren't going to be here."

"Obviously, I was able to make it, after all."

"What about your sons?"

"They're with my aunt for the moment."

"In California?"

His lips tightened a little. "I have the feeling that you're going to disapprove no matter how I answer."

Her approval or disapproval could hardly matter to Jake. "You're the one who said you had to get your sons squared away with another boarding school." Maybe all he'd done was delegate the task to his aunt. And he was obviously less surprised to see her there than she was to see him. "I suppose you've spoken with Miguel." It wasn't really a question, but Jake still nodded.

And if he'd have had anything else to add, J.D. would never know, because Dr. Windsor did return then. The tired smile the surgeon gave was only slightly encouraging. "We've pinned what we could and removed a few fragments that were crushed beyond repair. In that regard, the surgery's a success, though his prognosis is still poor. We've moved him to the recovery pool now."

J.D. knew that Latitude would be suspended by a sling into a water-cushioned limbo, minimizing his chances of reinjuring himself as he regained consciousness. After that, the next step would be to keep him from reinjuring himself when he was *out* of the pool.

Every step, literally, would be a test. And each test would be performed on the tightrope of preventing some other complication because horses, despite their immense size, possessed extremely complicated systems.

"It'll still be another hour or two before we know more," the surgeon continued. "Go and get something to eat. Some rest. We'll call."

Jake thanked him and the surgeon headed out again.

J.D., though, hurried after him. "Dr. Windsor, is it possible for me to go back to the pool area?"

His eyes narrowed for a moment. "I'll see what I can arrange."

"Thank you."

Angel came up behind J.D. "Do you think that's wise?" Her voice was soft. "Latitude could thrash around. That's a half ton of horse flesh. If you get too near him—" her eyebrows lifted meaningfully "—need I elaborate?"

"I'll keep a safe distance away," J.D. promised.

Her sister looked skeptical. "And when have you ever been able to keep your distance from a horse in distress?"

"Things are different now." Her gaze went past Angel to Jake who was watching them closely. But she knew he couldn't have overheard their whispered exchange.

She slowly returned to the waiting area. "I hope you don't mind." Her hand moved awkwardly. "That I asked to be allowed into recovery."

His dark eyes seemed to study her even more closely. "Why would I mind?"

"I'm not with Forrest's Crossing anymore. I probably should have run it by you first."

"Probably," he agreed. "But about what I expected. You and that colt—" He shook his head slightly. "I have some business to take care of, but I'll send my driver back for you. You and your sister can join me later for dinner."

"Oh, but—"

"Thank you, Jake," Angeline spoke smoothly over J.D. "That's very kind of you."

"But I don't think—"

"It's the least I can do." He seemed to have the same desire to speak over J.D.'s protests. "Did you already arrange accommodations for the night?"

Aggravated with the both of them, J.D. crossed her arms and named the usual hotel that his stable crew used—on the rare occasions when they'd bothered with a hotel at all.

"I'll arrange rooms for you at the Plaza where I'm staying, instead."

"I want to stay near Latitude," J.D. countered evenly.

His expression tightened a little. "I'm well aware of where your priorities lay. I'll ensure that you have access to my driver so you can come and go as you please."

"But—"

Angeline closed her arm around J.D.'s shoulder, her hand squeezing. "I've always wanted to stay at the Plaza," she said amicably.

J.D. hadn't wanted to pinch her sister so badly since Angel let slip to their ninth-grade class that J.D. had a crush on the history teacher.

"Then consider it done." Jake smiled, annoyingly satisfied as he addressed Angeline, almost as if J.D. weren't even there. "Until later, then."

Her teeth were nearly gnashing together as he strode away. "Until later, then," she repeated under her breath once he was gone. "You are married, you know," she reminded crossly. "With a baby on the way."

Angel laughed right out loud. "Good Lord, J.D. You do have it bad."

"I don't have *it* bad." But she realized the more she protested, the more it sounded as if she did. "I'm not in love with Jake Forrest," she said softly. Distinctly. "I had sex with him once." Amazing sex. World class sex. "That's all."

"Keep telling yourself that." Angeline's tone was humorous. She tucked her arm through J.D.'s and steered her around until she was no longer staring after the spot that Jake had vacated. "Just remember what resulted from that singular incident. You've got a baby on the way, too, and maybe as a concerned sister, I think it's my duty to get to know the daddy a little better."

"He wasn't even supposed to be here!" She was appalled at the way her emotions careened inside her.

"Well, he is," Angel pointed out gently, "and frankly, the man seems exceedingly gracious."

"It's an act," J.D. muttered. "A warm, honey-smooth Southern *act*. The man wants something."

"What if what he wants is you?"

She ignored the hop-skip-and-a-jump inside her. "The only thing he wants from me has to do with Latitude."

"Are you certain?"

"Believe me. I couldn't be further from his type if I tried."

Angel lifted her eyebrows. "And yet," she waved her hand slightly. "Look what happened."

J.D. made a face. Sex wasn't the same thing as a relationship. She'd already learned that lesson thanks to Donny and Troy. And she'd proven with them that she wasn't the forever-after type. And when it came to her baby, whether Jake wanted her or not was immaterial because she never wanted her child to look at him with that combination of agonizing yearning and pained acceptance the way that Zach and Connor looked at him. She couldn't bear it.

"Ms. Clay?" A young woman wearing pink surgical scrubs appeared. "Dr. Windsor said I should take you back to the pool."

A different brand of nervousness shot through her. J.D. looked at Angel. "I didn't think to ask if you minded waiting even longer."

Her sister shooed her. "I'll be fine. I want to call Brody anyway. You just be *very* careful."

The fact that J.D. had a reason to *be* very careful was still something that she found hard to believe. "I will."

As it turned out, none of them had needed to worry about Latitude's reaction to coming out of his anesthesia. Like the trouper that he was, he remained calm and cooperative, while blindfolded and blanketed, with tubes running here and there, he was hoisted out of the odd raft-shaped contraption and slowly, carefully, maneuvered around until he was settled on his feet. His injured limb was heavily bandaged. A special horseshoe had been placed on his right hind hoof to help offset the weight and height of the bandages on his left.

He was as still as he could be, and J.D. knew that he sensed he had to be. And when they slowly walked him the short distance to a stall and his blindfold was finally removed, she didn't bother trying to hold back her tears when he butted his head against her shoulder, nearly tearing right through the sterile gown she'd been given to wear before entering the pool area. "I'd feed you peppermints all night if I could." She stroked his cheek. "Such a brave boy."

He huffed at that and she smiled a little and pressed her lips against his nose.

"He's probably protesting the *boy* bit," Jake's voice came from behind her.

Her bootie-covered shoes slipped when she whirled around to face him.

"Whoa." Jake's arm shot out and caught her shoulder, stopping her slide. "You all right?"

Aside from shaking all over? "Fine," she lied. "I didn't expect you to come back."

"Lat is my horse." His reminder was mild. "I finished earlier than expected and wanted to see how he was doing."

He wore a disposable gown similar to hers over his trousers and shirt, though his gown was considerably tighter across his shoulders.

She turned her gaze to safer regions. Namely Latitude. "He's doing great."

"Hmm." Jake's arm brushed against her as he reached around her to run his hand over the colt's head. "He's in for a long recuperation."

"Yes." She inched away. "I should get back to my sister. It's been a long day for us both."

"I saw her in the waiting room. I put her in a cab back to the hotel already. As you said, it's been a long day and she was almost asleep in her chair out there."

Guilt swamped her. Her sister had been incredibly supportive. But she had good reason, herself, to be exhausted. "Thank you," she forced out the words.

His brown gaze slanted down at her. "It just about chokes you to say that, doesn't it?"

Her cheeks heated, but there was no point in denying what was so plainly obvious. "I'm sorry. I just find it difficult to accept your generosity when there's no—"

In a flash, his hand had moved from stroking Latitude's head, to pressing a long finger over her lips. "There's reason. One very good reason."

Her mouth ran dry. She couldn't see well enough past his thick, spiky lashes to read his hooded gaze. "What?" His finger felt warm and intimate as she formed the word.

"I'm sure you know." He drew his finger downward until the tip tugged gently against the very center of her lower lip.

The stall gate was a welcome support against her.

He couldn't possibly know about the baby.

Just because Angeline had figured it out on her own didn't mean that Jake would have, too. "N-no."

"I want you to come back and work with Latitude."

Her tension escaped like a stuck balloon, leaving her feeling just as deflated.

Of course he meant Latitude. What else?

Chapter Seven

Jake wasn't accustomed to the tension he felt, waiting for J.D.'s answer.

And when it came, she didn't even look him in the face. "I can't." She pressed her hands together. "I've told you that."

"Can't? Or won't?"

She ducked beneath his shoulder. Latitude's head shifted, his dark, solemn eyes tracking her.

"Can't," she repeated. "I've bought a small spread in Weaver. I'm boarding horses."

He lifted his brows. "That was quick. You've been gone from Forrest's Crossing for only two weeks." He could have calculated it down to days, hours and maybe even minutes if she'd asked.

Not that he intended on admitting that particular point. It was his own damn fault that he missed her presence more acutely than he'd expected.

Her cheeks were rosy. "It *was* quick. But I found the right property at the right time and saw no reason to wait. The owner was as anxious to sell as I was to buy. And when I can afford it, I'll buy the adjoining property, too."

"Setting down roots in a big hurry."

She lifted her shoulder. "So? I haven't had roots—" she sketched air quotes with her fingers "—in a long time." Her eyes met his, strangely intense. "I'm thirty-one. I'm not getting any younger. It's…time."

His nape prickled a little. "Now you're sounding like my sister Charlotte. She's either begging for more responsibilities at Forco or moaning about time running out for her to have children. One of these days she'll learn she can't have both."

"Why not?"

"So she can be a parent like I am? Kids take time. Forco doesn't leave any. Next thing you'll be telling me is that *your* biological clock is ticking."

Her chin lifted. "What if it…was?"

"Then I wish you luck settling down with some good old rancher boy." The fact that he'd want to destroy said rancher boy was beside the point.

"Ah." Her lips twisted. She looked away. "As it happens, I'm not looking for a husband. Just a place to call my own. And now that I've found one, I don't intend to leave it."

"Not even for Latitude?" He didn't wait for an answer. "You'd have to be boarding a helluva lot of horses to make what I'm willing to pay you. Think what you could do with the money at this place you call your own."

"Not everything is about money."

His lips tensed. "Everything is about money." He'd learned that when he was a kid and the mother who claimed to want him and his sisters so badly had settled instead for a hefty chunk of money before she'd skipped on down the road.

"Is that the only reason you're spending money to fix Latitude's leg?"

"Of course. He may not race again—probably won't—but he's got to be able to stand at stud."

The registration of thoroughbreds was tightly monitored and for a foal to be registered—among other requirements—it had to be the product of a physical mating. Which meant the stallion had to be physically capable of mounting a broodmare.

"And if he can't, the insurance covering him against catastrophes like this is worth far more than he is." She looked up at him as if he'd somehow let her down.

"I don't invest in a horse for the pleasure of watching him graze in a pasture. I expect a return." He lifted his hand. "And before you start arguing with me, I'm already well aware that you disagree."

"So, what happens if Latitude's leg doesn't heal perfectly?" Her chin came up. "What if he develops complications?"

"What do you want me to say, J.D.? That I won't, under any circumstances, look at euthanasia?" If a horse couldn't distribute his weight evenly among his four legs, a host of difficulties could arise—some even fatal. "Would you want to condemn Lat to a life of pain?"

She looked ill. "No. But if pain isn't an issue, and he still can't race, and he still can't mount a mare, then—"

"—then what good is he to me?"

She winced. "So, sell him to me." She reached out and closed her hands over Jake's arm, seeming to surprise herself just as much as she did him. "Sell him to me right now."

"J.D., you know how expensive it was to just get Lat through today's surgery?" For him, the money was insignificant. But for her? "Surgery's just the start if his recuperation isn't textbook perfect."

"I don't care." Her voice was soft. Passionate. "I'm not indigent, Jake. I have *some* means."

He knew that she came from a very successful ranching

family but he also knew it wasn't likely they had the kind of resources that he did.

And he knew what she'd been earning working for him for the past five years.

He closed his hands over hers and squeezed gently. "You just said you bought a house, J.D. You won't work with Latitude even if it profits you. But do you really want to chance putting your entire future in financial straits? How much do you want to stretch yourself?"

Her eyes glistened. "I don't care how far into debt it puts me."

"You'd buy him no matter how financially unsound it would be. But you won't come back to work with him."

Her lips parted but she didn't answer. Her lashes swept down, hiding her eyes.

His jaw felt tight. "No. The real problem is that you won't come back to work with *me*. That's what it all keeps coming back down to."

"I told you that my coming to see Latitude now wouldn't change that."

"This is because we slept together."

She looked pained. "Jake—"

"Isn't it? What is it you don't want to face about that night? The fact that you enjoyed it so much?"

Her hand lifted and he caught her wrist before her palm could reach his cheek. She stared at him, her fingers curling.

"Pardon me. I need to check on Latitude."

The third voice was jarringly intrusive.

He yanked his gaze away from J.D. to look at the source.

It was Dr. Bowen, the resident veterinarian.

Jake let out a breath and slowly released J.D. then moved away to make room for the other man to step into the stall.

He didn't miss the way she tucked her hands around her waist as if to make certain he couldn't touch her again.

His jaw tightened until it ached.

"Let's see if you're feeling hungry, eh, Latitude?" The young veterinarian's voice was cheerful as he filled Latitude's feed bag.

J.D. anxiously watched, but a smile touched her lips when the colt impatiently shoved past the vet to get at the feed. Her gaze flicked up to Jake and hung there for a moment. But then she moistened her lips and looked away again. "My sister probably thinks I've completely abandoned her. I should get going."

That's the way she was going to play it, then.

He tamped down the urge to push and it was harder than it should have been. "My driver is still here, waiting."

She looked as if she wanted to refuse the ride, but after a moment, she nodded. She gave Latitude a long hug and then she and Jake left the stall area. They disposed of their paper gowns and booties, and headed out into the dark evening.

As soon as they appeared, his limo pulled away from its spot beneath a lamppost and stopped almost at their feet. Jake pulled open the rear door and waited for J.D. to climb inside.

In seconds, the car swept out of the parking lot.

She stared out the side window at the flickering lights they passed and *he* stared at her. There was soft music coming from the speakers. But the low, mournful sax only seemed to underscore the silence.

"Your aunt has her hands full, I imagine, with the boys." Her voice was still tight and she didn't look away from the window. "How is their mother doing?"

"She's had several rounds of surgery already." Talking about his ex-wife was the last thing he wanted to do, but at least it filled the thick silence that he knew he was to blame for. "She probably has more pins in her bones than Latitude does." What would worry Tiffany, though, was how well she'd be able to get rid of the scars.

"But she will recover, right?"

"Depends on your definition of recovery."

Her chin angled around and her gaze burned over him. "She'll live."

"Yes."

"And so will Latitude."

He studied the profile she'd presented again, noticing—not for the first time—just how delicate her features were. "Is that just faith or intentionally positive thinking?"

"Is there a lot of difference?"

"You're asking the wrong person. I don't believe in faith."

"If you had no faith, you'd have never put Latitude through the surgery in the first place." She looked at him again. "Miguel told me the track vet advised putting him down. Your sister agreed. Miguel agreed. You could have consented, collected the insurance, end of story. Nobody would have blamed you."

She would have blamed him. He knew it as certainly as he knew his own name.

"Tell that to the animal rights group that was parked outside the gates at Forrest's Crossing within an hour of the race."

Her brows drew together. "Seriously?"

"Mabel told me when they arrived. They were still there when I got home, all ready to draw and quarter me as an example of the cruelty of the industry. Imagine what they'd have had to say if Latitude had shared Sideofhoney's fate?"

"You've never cared what reporters had to say."

"Only if it affects the P & L at Forco."

Her lips firmed. "I refuse to believe you're guided only by money. You're going to extraordinary means to save Latitude."

"I wasn't willing to give up on the possibility yet that he could still produce," he said flatly. "It's a calculated risk."

"Call it what you want. Somewhere, you had faith that he could still be a winner—whether on a racetrack or in the breeding shed."

He shook his head at her. "You like putting a pretty slant on it."

"And you're determined to be cynical and jaded. Why is that?"

His laughter was short and devoid of humor. "Well, honey, that is because I am my father's son."

And because he *was,* looking at J.D. and thinking of anything beyond the horse they had in common was pure fantasy.

When they arrived at the hotel, the concierge, Diana, was waiting for him with his key and messages. "You're in your usual suite, Mr. Forrest."

He barely slowed to take the messages and tucked his hand behind J.D.'s back, guiding her to the elevators.

Once inside, he handed her one of the keycards. "Your and your sister's suite is on the seventeenth floor."

"Suite!" She looked startled as she took the card. "Jake, that really wasn't—" She broke off when he tiredly lifted his hand. "Thank you," she finished instead. "Where are you?"

"A few floors up." He pulled out the messages again and paged through them, but his mind wasn't really on the contents.

His usual suite would be comfort itself.

And it would also be silent.

Empty.

"They know you pretty well here," she commented after a moment.

"Hmm." He glanced at her. Something was ticking behind those brown eyes.

"Even Diana?"

He hid his surprise as he absorbed that. Diana was lovely and had never made a secret of her availability if he'd have been interested.

His tastes though, had become wholly centered on a certain green-eyed blonde with a mile-wide stubborn streak.

Frankly, it annoyed the hell out of him. "Who?"

Her soft lips tightened just as the elevator softly chimed.

"This is my floor." She stated the obvious, and stuck one foot out, as if she were afraid the car might keep on moving if she weren't careful. "And if you don't mind, I'll take a rain check on the dinner. I'm too worn out to eat."

A rain check she had no intention of redeeming, he'd be willing to bet. "Another time, then."

The relief on her face was almost comical. And it was proof that he wasn't any sort of gentleman by enjoying the unease that followed hard on the heels of that relief when he stopped off the elevator with her. "I'll walk you to your room."

"I'm not in danger of getting lost," she muttered, striding ahead of him. She reached the door and swiped the key card, but he smoothly pushed open the door for her and walked inside.

J.D. was eyeing him suspiciously as she slowly entered the quiet room. "My sister *is* here, right?"

"In there, I imagine." He gestured at a door that was closed on the other side of the beautifully appointed living area. "Which leaves that room for you." He nodded at the opened doorway behind them through which they could see a massively wide, king-size bed.

The image of the two of them sharing it filled his head with agonizing clarity.

The price to be paid, he supposed, for deliberately needling her out of her comfort zone.

She backed toward the door and moistened her lips, which only succeeded in drawing his attention right to them. "It's a beautiful room and much too generous of you. But thank you."

"You're welcome." He could still see the corner of that king-size bed and judging by the way she clenched her hand over the door handle, he figured she did, too.

"Well. Good night."

He stopped next to her. "What? No handshake? No hug?"

She shot him a look. "Very funny."

"Nobody from the stable around here to gossip, so why are you so nervous?"

"I'm not nervous. I'm tired."

His head ducked over hers. "Liar." He whispered the accusation against her ear.

She jerked her head back. "If you want to amuse yourself, call down to Diana. I'm sure she'd be accommodating." Her voice was thin. But there was a fiery glint in her eyes that he found a whole lot more interesting.

He settled his hand on her shoulder. He knew her slenderness was deceptive. He'd seen for himself how she could control a half ton of racing horseflesh.

How she could control *him* with the slightest flex of her hips.

"That's twice now," he murmured. "Are you jealous, J.D.?"

She rolled her eyes. "Don't be ridiculous."

"That's right." He tilted his head, studying her. "The thing that gets your blood pumping is Latitude." He waited for her to deny it.

Wished that she would.

But all she did was look away, the sooty fringe of her eyelashes throwing shadows on her ivory cheeks. "You should go."

Truer words had never been spoken. "I haven't been able to, you know."

Her forehead crinkled a little. She finally lifted her lashes, curiosity obviously getting the better of her. "Excuse me?"

"Forget," he supplied. "I haven't been able to forget." Then he lowered his head and covered her mouth in a fast, hard kiss.

But when he lifted his head, he wasn't sure just who had been seared.

She stared at him, her lips softly parted. And before he could do something really crazy—like pull her into that room with that waiting bed—he yanked open the door and walked away.

Chapter Eight

There wasn't much about the town of Weaver, Wyoming, that called attention to itself as Jake drove slowly down the main street with its curbs covered by plowed snow.

A diner named Ruby's that looked like it was doing a brisk business; a couple of shops; a couple more restaurants; a sprawling old motel. If he'd been driving faster than a snail's pace, he'd have passed by them all in the blink of an eye.

The GPS unit in his dash told him he had just another ten miles before he reached J.D.'s place, and it annoyed the hell out of him that the closer he got, the more he had to restrain himself from hitting the gas pedal a little harder.

He hadn't spoken with her in weeks. Not since that night in her hotel suite when he'd had to force himself to walk away from her.

If he'd have stayed with her for two seconds longer, he'd have had her in that bedroom and kept her there for a month of Sundays no matter how wrong he knew it would have been.

Instead, he'd been short-tempered at the business meeting he'd had early the next morning, and blown off two other appointments to drive out to the equine center. But when he'd expected to find her there with Latitude, he'd been stunned to learn that she hadn't shown up there that day at all.

She and her sister had checked out of the hotel and returned to Wyoming without a single word to him.

The thin vein of decency inside him said it was only what he deserved after the way he'd kissed her. But he'd still taken juvenile delight in shredding the concise and formal little thank you note she'd later sent, and tossing the pieces in the fireplace.

And now, here he was.

Hauling the damn colt to *her* because he'd finally accepted the fact that she wasn't coming back to Georgia no matter what.

The small detail of not having *notified* her that he was bringing Latitude to her was immaterial.

It had been a long drive from the Cheyenne airport, where he and Latitude had flown into. And that had been followed by the involved process of moving the colt from his private jet to the specially outfitted horse trailer that Sidney had arranged to have waiting.

His sister thought he was insane going to such effort for the horse, but she'd still been a help when he'd needed her to be. In that, she was more like J.D. than she would probably ever admit.

The dulcet female voice on his GPS told him to turn at the next intersection, and he followed. The route took him through what was obviously a newer area of town. There was a sizable apartment complex; a modest, but decent-sized shopping center. A few chain restaurants and another motel.

He turned again when the GPS directed, and he quickly left behind even those fresher marks of Weaver progress for a sweeping arch of narrow, but smoothly paved road that snaked out into the open snow-covered plains.

The road crested slightly, and he figured he didn't need confirmation from Madame GPS to guess that the only dwelling that came into view was J.D.'s.

The house sat well back from the road. It was two-storied and modestly sized, and its white paint and black shutters looked freshly done.

When he drove up the gravel drive that ended on one side of the house, he had a clearer sight of the faded red barn situated behind the house, as well as the unpainted wood fencing that surrounded several corrals where a few horses stood around grazing through the trampled snow.

Everything looked on the long side of well used.

And it was all a helluva far cry from the rolling acres surrounded by pristine, white fencing that he was used to at Forrest's Crossing.

It was also as cold as a witch's temper and for a moment he had a second of doubt about what he was doing.

How could Latitude turn the corner toward a recovery in a place like this? Even *with* J.D.?

But then he saw her familiar figure, her lankiness hidden beneath the bulky jacket that reached all the way down to her knees, walking from the barn area toward the house.

He knew the moment she spotted him, because she went stock still.

The only thing that moved was her curling blond hair, longer than ever, drifting around her arms in the cold breeze, and the visible puffs of breath circling around her head.

He shoved his cold hands in his pockets and blessed the heated truck and horse trailer as he started toward J.D., closing the distance between them.

Her emerald eyes were narrowed against the sunlight that seemed inordinately bright thanks to the reflection against the snow. Her coat was an ugly blue-and-red check, her jeans were muddy from the calves down, and there wasn't a speck of makeup on her ivory face. The red on her nose and her cheeks was clearly caused by the cold.

And damned if he wasn't instantly primed and ready for her, just as he had been that night at the hotel.

One hint that she'd be receptive would be all it took.

But receptiveness wasn't anywhere in evidence when she stopped several feet away, and he figured it was just as well.

She was still the kind of woman good men wanted to marry, and he was still the kind of man who ought to know enough to stay miles away.

It was his own damned luck that she seemed more beautiful than ever.

"Jake," she finally greeted, after giving the truck and trailer parked near her house a thorough look.

"J.D.," he returned in the same even tone.

Her gaze glanced off his. "I don't suppose that trailer is empty."

"Don't suppose it is."

Her lips thinned. "You have a colossal ego." But he could still see the way her gaze kept creeping back toward the horse trailer.

"It's been almost six weeks since the accident." His voice was even. "Lat's cast has been changed multiple times. He's battling an infection. He's been off his feed and actually bit Miguel."

She drew her brows together, her gaze snapping back to him. "And you shipped him all the way here?" Her opinion was clear. He was mad to put an ailing horse through such an ordeal.

"*Here* is his last chance."

She paled to a shade not much more colorful than the stark white snow all around them. "Latitude needs a good vet. Not a former assistant trainer."

"Your cousin's husband is a good vet," he returned just as rapidly. Evan Taggart had an excellent reputation with large animals. He knew, because he'd checked. "Lat had a good vet back home, too. What he didn't have was you. I'll double the fee you were getting at Forrest's Crossing and pay for whatever supplies or equipment you think you'll need."

"I'm not going to argue fees with you. What you were paying me in Georgia was more than enough. And there's no need for expenses, anyway, because I'm not—"

"Consider it an investment in your future as a trainer," he interrupted. "Someday, the racing world can thank me."

She looked uncertain for a moment, only to shake her head firmly. "No. I'm finished with racing."

He lifted his brows, truly surprised. "Why? You were a natural."

She held his gaze for a long, tight moment. But she looked away first and her cheeks were rosier than ever. "We might as well get him into the barn." She pointed to a small clearing. "Pull the trailer up there."

Though he'd counted on her soft spot for Latitude, he was still relieved that she hadn't sent them straight back to the highway. He returned to the warmth of his truck and drove around to where she'd indicated, backing the trailer as close as possible to the barn doors that she'd pushed wide open. She was already lowering the rear gate when he joined her and he pulled open the trailer doors.

Inside, Latitude snorted and shifted nervously. J.D. quickly went in beside him, and the horse almost magically calmed. With practiced ease, she untied him and pushed aside the rump bar. "Come on, handsome," he heard her croon. "Back it up."

Lat took his time about it. But J.D. was patient. And eventually, the colt had backed down the shallow ramp. He resisted again the second his hoof hit snow-covered ground, but still, J.D. showed no impatience. She just waited until he was ready to move in his own time, and when he did, she rubbed her hands over him, praising him all the way toward the barn, and damned if Latitude's demeanor didn't noticeably pick up.

"There's a bushel of apples sitting inside the kitchen door. Would you mind going to get one?"

It wasn't very common for Jake to be put into the role of gopher, but he strode across the unyielding ground toward the house. The kitchen door was presumably the door that faced the barn. Up three steps, and he was inside a rectangular mudroom. There was a cord fastened on the walls running across the short end of the room. It was oddly old-fashioned to see a clothesline like that hanging above a state-of-the-art washer and dryer that rivaled the one at Forrest's Crossing.

What was most distracting, though, was the handful of lacy bras and skimpy panties hanging over the line. They brought to mind much too easily the memory of him stripping similar garments away from her satiny skin.

He continued through the mudroom into a kitchen that smelled like warm chocolate. There, he saw more new appliances. Fresh paint. Surprisingly contemporary and very inviting.

He grabbed a few apples out of the bushel that was, indeed, sitting on the floor just inside the doorway, and strode back outside.

She'd gotten Latitude inside the barn and was letting him sniff around, looking as curious as a kid in a toy store while she pitched fresh straw into an empty stall. "You might have given me some warning," she said without looking up at him, "about your plans."

"And chanced you leaving the state or the country?" He tossed the apples in the air, catching them one by one. "Don't think so."

Her head snapped up and she gave him a serious glare. "This is my home. Why would I leave it?"

"Forrest's Crossing was your home for a while, too, and you sure as hell left it."

She shoved her pitchfork into the bale and scattered more on to the stall floor. Her face was rosy, whether still from the

cold outside—her exertions now in the warmth of the barn—
or his comment, he couldn't tell.

"Forrest's Crossing is *your* home. I just worked there."
She poked and tossed and scattered some more, then straightened and pulled out a pocketknife. "If you're just going to
stand there, be useful and cut the apple. See if he'll eat it."
She balanced the knife on top of the stall rail and went back
to her pitchfork, almost as if she were afraid to chance
touching him by handing him the knife directly.

He unfolded the knife and deftly cut the apple in quarters.
Another horse—a handsome dappled gray—stuck his head
over his stall as if he scented the fruit, but Latitude showed
no interest.

Jake rubbed his hand over Lat's neck. "It's okay, bud." But
it wasn't. Not really. Next to those peppermints of J.D.'s, Lat
was a fiend for apples.

Jake finally went over to the gray and began feeding the
quarters to him. "How many horses do you have here?"

"Six. Five are boarding. They're all pretty good-natured.
Ziggy there is mine."

The gelding's ears swiveled at his name, but he was too
busy wolfing down the apple quarters to do much more than
that. "When'd you get him?"

"When I was seventeen. He's always been out at my
parents' place, but now that I have my own place…" She kept
working. "You might want to watch out for Bonneville next
to him. He likes to nip. He came just this week. His owners
are gonna dump him for a quick sale if I don't break him of
the habit."

Jake tossed the buckskin an apple quarter as he put a few
feet of distance between them. The stocky, muscular horse
snatched it mid-air.

"Was Ziggy your first?"

At that, she lifted her head, and something came and went

in her eyes. "My first horse was Bonita. My parents gave her to me for my twelfth birthday. She came out of my uncle's farm like Ziggy there. We were almost as inseparable as Angeline and I were."

"Were?"

She jabbed her pitchfork into the straw, returning to her task. "My father put her down when I was seventeen."

Her voice was even, her tone practical. But he was beginning to recognize a particular nuance within that combination—and knew that there was a lot of emotion shifting around beneath that smooth surface. "Why?"

"She got spooked by a rattler and threw me. The snake managed to bite her a few times." Her movements slowed. "She was in a panic and ended up shattering several bones before she stomped the snake to death."

"Were *you* hurt?"

Her shoulder lifted and her movements quickened again. "She ended up stomping me a few times in the process, but she kept the snake from getting at me."

He had a very vivid memory of kissing his way along a faint scar low on her belly. At the time, they'd both been more interested in other matters than the history behind her scar, but now he was imagining her, as a girl, trying to escape the dangerous hooves of a terrified horse. "Stomping you how badly?"

Her gaze lifted to his and she looked about ready to say something, only to close her mouth again. "I recovered," she finally said briskly. "Bonita obviously didn't. The next summer, I picked out Ziggy. He's a good ol' boy. Even tempered. Eager to please." She poked the pitchfork back into the straw, punctuating the end of the subject.

Jake looked around the barn. There were eight stalls running down the center. A couple more built against one of the outer walls. The one she was preparing for Latitude was closest to the barn door. "Your barn looks bigger than your house."

"Lot of 'em are around here. Gotta have a pretty successful spread to sink needless money into personal comfort." She evidently deemed the straw bed finally satisfactory, because she stuck the pitchfork back on a peg inside the tack area, filled Latitude's water, then went over to him, coaxing him with soft murmurs into the stall. While the colt gingerly stepped around the new space and tried nibbling at the collar of her coat, she used the knife Jake had returned to her to cut the other apple in pieces and slowly, patiently, talked him into taking two.

Jake figured he was a sad case when he was jealous of the affectionate praise she bestowed so easily on his horse.

She was plainly pleased when she finally stepped out of the stall and closed the gate. Pleased that was until she addressed Jake without really looking at him. "You might as well come in the house," she said in a tone that said she wasn't thrilled with the idea. "Please tell me that you didn't drive Latitude all the way from Forrest's Crossing."

"We flew into Cheyenne and drove from there."

She looked only slightly less disapproving. "What if I hadn't been here?"

"But you were." He wasn't stupid enough to tell her that he'd checked on her to make certain that she was, indeed, exactly where he'd expected her to be. Where she'd been every day since she'd bought the place, using up nearly every speck of savings she'd possessed in the process.

"Never mind the fact that I might have had plans today." She pushed the barn door closed when they were on the other side of it with more force than was probably necessary. "Must be nice to have the world always accommodating itself for you." Her long legs began eating up the distance toward the house.

He let out a snort as he easily kept pace with her. "Oh, hell yeah. Everything falling into place *for* me. That would explain my mother walking out on me and my sisters when we were kids. My selfish bastard of a father. Tiff's defection. Even yours, for that matter."

She stopped dead still. "I didn't *defect*."

"You left us when we needed you most." Story of his life, when he thought about it. Which he usually didn't, since he'd learned long ago that wishing for something never changed what was.

Her hands had gone to the hips of her thick jacket and temper snapped in her eyes. "Do you hold such a grudge against all of the Forrest's Crossing employees who've had the nerve to quit? Or am I just special that way?"

His gaze dropped to her lips and she seemed to realize it about the same time that he did, because those soft lips went into a tight little line and she whirled around, crossing the gravel with even quicker steps.

She darted up the back steps and yanked open the door, disappearing inside without a single glance back at him. He was almost surprised to find she hadn't tried locking him out when he followed her through the mudroom and into the welcome warmth of the kitchen where she was washing her hands at the sink.

He realized the source of the chocolate aroma when she whipped a white-and-blue dishtowel off the pan it was covering on the counter. She wielded a knife over the pan, then scooped out neat squares onto a white plate and didn't speak until she was finished. "Do you want a brownie?"

His mouth was pretty much watering and it was definitely not for the chocolate dessert. "No, thanks."

"Good." She snapped off a length of plastic wrap and covered the plate. "There's barely enough for dinner as it is. And thanks to you, I'm already running late."

"For what?"

"My plans that you interrupted." She finally turned to look at him, bracing her hands on the edge of the counter behind her. "Dinner. Obviously. When is your flight back to Georgia?"

"Here's your hat, what's your hurry? You that anxious to get rid of me?"

"Of course not." Her steady gaze didn't flinch at the obvious lie.

"Don't worry. I won't interfere with your dinner plans." Though he wanted to know who exactly she was baking brownies for. "But I don't have a flight to catch. Not anytime soon."

Something shifted in her eyes. "What's that supposed to mean?"

"I didn't come here just to dump off Latitude on you. I'm staying with him."

"I can't see you bedding down in the barn with him," she scoffed, but that something in her eyes had coalesced into outright alarm.

"I saw a few hotels driving through town." From the cars parked outside of them, neither looked in danger of being overbooked.

"Motels," she corrected. "And while both are perfectly clean and acceptable, neither is at all close to the kind of accommodations that you're used to."

"I'm not expecting the Plaza."

"That's a good thing, because you're not going to get anything remotely close. No swimming pools. No business centers. No spas. No gazillion-starred restaurant. Satellite television is about the newest comfort of home that either one is offering."

"I'm not here to watch television."

"Then what *are* you here to watch? If you don't trust me with Latitude, why on earth did you bring him here in the first place?"

"You know damned well that I trust you. But I'm not going back until he's either truly recovering, or—"

"Not," she finished in a clipped tone. "And how much time are you allotting from your precious schedule for Latitude to prove whether or not he deserves to live?"

His jaw felt tight. "As much time as it takes."

Her eyes narrowed. "That could be months."

"Then I'll be here for months." His office was used to him conducting business from the road because of his frequent travels. Of course, those travels were ordinarily textile related, but that was beside the point. "I don't expect it'll take that long, though. At the rate that Latitude has been declining, it's not going to take all that long for him to get to such a bad stage that—"

"Don't even say it." She lifted her hand as if to ward off the words. "Thanksgiving is in just a few weeks."

"So?"

She blinked. "So? Don't your sons have a school break for the holiday?"

"Yeah, and they'll be at Tiff's place in San Francisco."

"She's out of the hospital, then?"

"No. But Lupe's there. Tiffany's housekeeper," he provided at her blank look.

She was clearly appalled. "They should be with family."

"Lupe will take them to see Tiffany at the hospital. It's what Tiffany wants," he added.

"What about what the boys want? Or what *you* want?" She waved her hand. "I'm not saying that they shouldn't see their mother, but surely it would be better if you were there." Her gaze was searching. "Don't you *want* to see them, Jake?"

"Thanksgiving is just another day out of the year in my family. The boys will have the long weekend at home with Lupe spoiling them rotten, they'll have dinner with their mother, then head back to Penley again."

"Penley! But I thought they were expelled after the lab accident."

The goo explosion had been no accident, which she knew, but he let it stand. "Enough money erases even an expulsion." Even aided by his aunt's charming attempts, he'd been unable to get them into any other suitable school. It had cost him a lot to get them back into Penley. But now there'd be a new wing of the library dedicated to the generosity of the Forrest family.

J.D. looked like she wanted to say more, but instead, she ran her hand over her head, tangling her fingers through her hair. "I'm a mess," she murmured, then sent him a sighing glance. "I guess you might as well come to dinner, too. Room service isn't on the menu at the motels, either. And heaven help me if they find out I didn't show you some Weaver hospitality."

"They?"

"My family." She picked up the plate of brownies and held them in front of her like a shield. "*You* can explain to my mother why we're late."

"Your family," he repeated, feeling abruptly wary. The last time he'd met a woman's family it had been his ex-wife's upon their engagement. It had been more like a business merger meeting than anything.

And the fact that he drew any comparisons between that relationship and J.D. wasn't something he was anxious to study very closely.

"Yes. My family. Something wrong with that?" She'd lifted an eyebrow and was watching him as if she could read every single thought in his mind. As if she expected him to back away from the very idea of it.

Which meant, of course, that he couldn't.

He smiled slowly, enjoying a little too much the way her pupils dilated with her own sense of alarm. "Not at all," he assured her. "In fact, I think it'll be very interesting."

The smile she gave was pinched. "Lovely."

Chapter Nine

Since the horse trailer was still hooked up to Jake's truck, J.D. had a good reason to insist on driving out to her parents' place where that week's Sunday dinner was being held. And, if she was driving her own truck, they could leave whenever she wanted.

For her, that couldn't come too quickly. She didn't want Jake spending a minute more than necessary with her family, lest they start drawing unwanted conclusions.

She'd told them she was pregnant only a few weeks ago and as she'd expected, once their shocked surprise passed, they were all supportive and delighted at the idea of another baby in the family.

It had annoyed her father to no end, though, when she'd refused to talk about who the baby's father was. And *where* the baby's father was, for that matter.

Men who didn't honor their responsibilities when it came to their offspring was something that Daniel Clay still felt strongly about. It was one of the reasons why he'd been such a wonderful father when J.D.'s biological father had abandoned Maggie and her.

Not that J.D. had any particular memory of Joe Green. She'd been a baby when he'd left and to her, he was just a name. But she knew the facts and, even though she'd never had a reason to grieve over his abandonment or his death a few years later, she'd come to realize that some things were just inherited no matter how much she'd wished otherwise. Daniel was the only father that had ever mattered to J.D., but she knew it was from Joe Green that she'd gotten the faulty faithful gene. When it came to Daniel and Maggie, they were as true as true could be.

J.D.'s mother had been the one to get Daniel off his riled high horse when he'd demanded to know about the guy who'd gotten his little girl pregnant.

But J.D. was acutely aware that even though they were kindly allowing her some privacy over the matter, they were still full of questions and wanting answers.

As a result, walking through the side entrance of the home where she'd grown up—with Jake on her heels—was one of the most awkward moments of her entire life.

Not surprisingly, they immediately ran into all of J.D.'s aunts, who were in the kitchen along with her mother. She quickly stuck out the plate of brownies, rapidly plowing through the introductions that would only have to be repeated again when she encountered her father and the rest of the family. "Jake's brought Latitude to stay with me for a while," she finished, hoping that would be the end of it, considering they all knew her feelings about the colt.

Immediately, Jake was welcomed into the kitchen. J.D.'s aunt Emily took his jacket and Jaimie tucked her arm through his, drawing him farther into the house as she and J.D.'s other aunt, Rebecca, peppered him with questions about Latitude's condition.

Maggie, though, just held the tray of brownies and eyed J.D.

"I didn't know he was coming," J.D. said quickly, "or I'd have given you some notice that there'd be another seat at the table."

"You know adding another seat is hardly cause for alarm around here."

She did. There were times when they had upwards of thirty people around the family's weekly dinner table. And sometimes when they had only six. It all just depended on who was around and available. "Well, anyway, that's why I didn't have a chance to change into something more presentable."

"The mud on the jeans *is* a bit much," Maggie murmured. She finally set the plate of brownies on the counter where it joined a pie and a tray of cookies. "But we've all seen you in worse. Go on in. Squire and Jefferson have both been champing at the bit to talk to you about some mare they're having trouble with."

J.D. started out of the kitchen. "I'd just as soon Jake not hear about the baby," she said casually. "He might worry that working with Latitude would be too much."

She'd rehearsed the comment in her head every mile of the drive from her place. There was nothing but truth in her words. There was also nothing but a big fat lie of omission, too.

Fortunately, her mother didn't pounce on that statement the way she'd been known to ferret out the occasional prevarication of J.D.'s while growing up.

But this wasn't a homework assignment that had been forgotten in favor of an afternoon horseback ride, and before her mother's usual discernment could see through her, she escaped into the family room.

Before the afternoon was over, J.D. lost any hope that her family wouldn't be enamored of Jake. It also became readily apparent that her pregnancy wasn't a topic of remote interest with him around.

For one thing, the fact that he'd brought Latitude all the

way out to J.D. made him a pretty decent guy right off the bat. Add in the way he charmed every female in her family from young Hannah Taggart—who didn't take to strangers easily at all—to Gloria Clay—whose ability to size up a person in two seconds rivaled that of her husband and J.D.'s grandfather, Squire. Given Jake's infernal ability to talk horses with her uncles, construction with her father, and most every other subject that could have conceivably come up, she almost believed that they were more interested in his presence at dinner than hers!

She wasn't even able to leave at a reasonable hour. Her father had rolled out his blueprints for an addition he was set on building and he and Jake perused them for at least an hour.

Finally, she used Latitude as an excuse to tear them all apart. It wasn't a false excuse, either. She did want to check on the horse as it had been several hours since they'd settled him in the barn.

"Jake," Maggie offered as they headed to the door, "we have plenty of room here if you'd like to stay. A room at the Sleep Tite is fine for a night or two, but it's hardly comfortable for much more than that. J.D. so enjoyed working with you in Georgia that it's the least we can do."

J.D. nearly choked but Jake shook his head, managing to look rueful and gracious and—damn it—attractive, all at the same time as he refused. "That's really kind of you, Maggie, but I'll be in and out a lot and at J.D.'s most of the day, anyway."

"Well, the offer is open if you change your mind." She bussed J.D.'s cheek. "Of course you'd have to be careful that Daniel doesn't try sticking a power tool in your hand."

Even J.D. managed to join in the laughter at that, but she quickly skipped down the steps out to her truck, only pausing to look back when her mother called her name. "Yes?"

"If you want me to go with you to your doctor's appointment next week, let me know." Her mother's expression was serene.

But J.D. knew with a sinking feeling that Maggie, like Angeline, had come to her own conclusions all too accurately. "Sure." She sketched a wave, and practically dived into her pickup and shoved the key into the ignition with a shaking hand.

Jake had barely climbed in beside her before she pulled away from the house, her tires slipping a little as she wheeled a sharp turn to head out to the highway.

"In a hurry?"

"Just to check on Latitude."

"What's the doctor appointment about?"

Her fingers flexed around the steering wheel. She was glad for the dark that was barely alleviated by the greenish glow from the dashboard lights. "That's kind of personal, don't you think?" She didn't wait for an answer. "It's just a checkup." That was true, too. But also a whopper considering what it *didn't* say.

The appointment was with her obstetrician.

Before he could ask anything else that would have her mountain of omissions growing even more, she asked him to run down everything that had been done to and for Latitude since his surgery.

Fortunately, that discussion easily consumed the duration of the trip back to her place.

True to his word, Jake stuck to J.D. while she checked on the horse, even going so far as to help round up the others that were out in the field, bringing them in for the night. But at last, when everyone was watered and bedded, and Latitude was contentedly munching on fresh hay, Jake unhitched the horse trailer and drove away in his fancy truck.

Exhausted on every level, J.D. went inside. She forced down a glass of milk, decided that tidying up the kitchen could wait another day, and dragged herself up to her bedroom. She fell asleep almost as soon as her head hit the pillow.

Unfortunately, she woke a few hours later in a sweat from an impossibly vivid dream featuring none other than Jake.

Not even in dreams could she escape him.

Going back to sleep proved impossible and she turned on the light and climbed out of bed. Her reflection in the mirror above the dresser looked back at her and she turned sideways, pulling the oversized T-shirt that she used in place of pajamas tight against her abdomen.

She was nearly sixteen weeks along now. Even when she wasn't swallowed in her enveloping winter sweaters, the small bulge of Jake's baby was barely evident.

She covered the bump with her palms.

Maybe she was wrong not to tell Jake. Maybe he *would* feel the joy that she felt.

The green eyes that stared back at her from the mirror were full of doubt and she turned away from her reflection. She pulled on boots and a coat and traipsed to the barn.

All the horses—including Latitude—were quiet. She went into the tack room and pulled down the saddle soap and set to work cleaning tack. Not exciting, but necessary. And it passed the hours until dawn when hunger had her heading back to the house.

The sight of the dark-haired man sitting at her kitchen table was completely unexpected. She nearly jumped out of her skin, at first thinking that Jake had presumptuously entered her house.

But she quickly realized that the man wasn't Jake at all. "Ryan," she gasped. "What on earth are you doing here?"

He lifted the mug sitting in front of him. "Drinking coffee. Here." Without rising, he shoved the other chair out with his boot. "You're not looking real steady on your feet."

"I can't imagine why," she returned, but slid into the chair. Since she'd started taking in horses, he'd come by occasionally. He'd hauled hay for her and fixed a few things, and then he'd disappear again, just as unexpectedly. This, though, was a first. "Are you all right?"

"Heard your old boss was in town." He peered at her over the edge of the mug. "Are *you* all right?"

"Peachy keen," she assured blithely. "Why wouldn't I be?"

"That would explain the coat and boots but no pants." His lips twisted a little. "You tell him about that baby you're having?"

She wasn't going to be sidetracked so easily, and particularly not into confirming whether or not Jake was the mystery father of her baby. No matter what Jake said, she figured it wouldn't be long before he chafed at the quiet life in Weaver and headed back to Georgia. "What's going on with you? You don't show up at the Sunday dinners. You're not working that anyone can tell. Everyone is concerned."

He sipped the hot brew. Slowly set the mug on the table again. "They don't need to be."

She leaned across the table, closing her hand over his arm. "Ryan, you've gotta admit this is a little strange, even for you. You're staying at the Sleep Tite Inn." The same motel that Jake had chosen. "You could have gotten coffee at Ruby's if that's all you wanted. It's practically next door."

"I want a job."

"Where?" Realization dawned when he cocked an eyebrow. "You mean…*here?*"

"Yeah."

"I can't afford to pay you." He had to be aware of that. Everyone in the family knew she was getting by, but not by much.

"I'm not looking for pay."

She fell back, utterly surprised. "Then what are you looking for?"

"Anything to keep my hands busy enough to keep my brain shut off." His voice was flat.

She studied him for a moment. He could have gone to either Matthew or Jefferson for work. They both were generally always in need of good hands. He also could have done construction for her father's company, or hit their other uncle, Tristan, up for a job doing just about anything at his video gaming company, Cee-Vid. And any one of those options would have come with a paycheck.

"The barn needs painting. I was going to wait until spring, but if you're really just looking for something to fill your time—"

"I am. Do you have the supplies?"

"Yes. Everything's stacked up in the garage."

"I'll start today." He pushed away from the table and grabbed up a battered coat. "You ought to lock your doors." He headed through the mudroom.

Still bemused, it was a moment before J.D. scrambled after him, darting down the steps. "Ryan—"

Whatever she thought she was going to say jammed in her throat, though, at the sight of Jake's pickup truck rolling to a stop next to where they'd left his horse trailer the day before.

Even Ryan stopped for a moment, looking surprised. But after that brief hesitation, he kept walking toward the detached garage between the house and the barn.

She saw the brief nod the two men exchanged, and when Jake headed her direction, she jolted into action, hurrying back into the house.

He followed all too quickly and seemed to share the same lack of need to announce himself that her cousin had. She hadn't even had time to drag on pants from the pile of laundry sitting on the washing machine.

"Good morning," she greeted as if she weren't half-naked beneath her coat, and feeling undone just from the sight of him. He always looked good, but in well-worn jeans and what appeared to be a brand new shearling coat, he was mouthwatering. "There's coffee if you're interested. Mugs are in the cupboard above the coffee maker." She brushed past him, intending to head upstairs.

But Jake closed his hand around her arm, stopping her. "Did he spend the night here?"

For a moment, she missed connecting the dots. Then realization set in. "Ryan?"

"Whatever the hell his name is."

She carefully twisted her arm out of his grip. "If he did, it's no concern of yours." She went to move around him again, but Jake sidestepped until his broad shoulders were filling the doorway blocking off her escape.

"Did he?" His voice was low and dangerous and she was appalled at the distinctly excited flutter she felt inside.

She lifted her chin. And even knowing that she shouldn't take such delight in turning her words back on him, she did. "Are you jealous, Jake?"

His expression looked tight. Annoyed. "Yes." She didn't even have time to draw breath before his head swooped and his mouth burned over hers.

She froze, but the heat of his kiss thawed her far too rapidly and even knowing how foolish it was, her arms slid up his mile-wide shoulders, tangling behind his neck.

She tasted the low sound that growled through his throat, and his arms swept around her, dragging her up tight against him. Delving beneath her coat, his hands found her hips, pressing them hard against him and she could have drowned in the desire that rushed through her, flooding away all the good reasons why they shouldn't be doing this. In that moment, all she wanted was for him to keep touching her; to fill her; complete her.

His hand closed over her breast, thumb unerringly finding the excruciatingly sensitive nipple through the nightshirt and prodding it into an even tighter frenzy. Her head fell back. She hauled in a breath over his name and gasped outright when he lifted her off her feet and set her on the kitchen table, settling between her bare thighs.

"You remember that night, don't you." His voice was a low rasp as his hands slid beneath her rear. "Just as much as I do."

"Every night." The admission was faint. The desire inside her coiled tighter. "Jake—please…"

His mouth covered hers, his tongue doing insane things to her senses. And when his hand slid between them, cupping her, she nearly arched right off the table.

He gently caught her earlobe between his teeth. His hand burned through her panties, stampeding her relentlessly toward the precipice and she shot off it blindly, exploding in midair.

His breath caressed her ear as she cried out, shuddering wildly. "Does he know you come so easily for another man like this?"

The words sank in.

She jerked, shoving him back with all the humiliated strength she could muster. But he was already straightening anyway. "I'm sure he couldn't care less." Her legs were shaking as she rolled off the table, and her voice was faint, but she couldn't help it. "That was my cousin. Ryan."

He didn't look mollified. "How close a cousin?"

She felt nearly crippled with desire but her knees managed to regain some stuffing. "Might as well be a brother. Now are you going to get out of my way, or not?"

He didn't move a muscle. "I don't like seeing you with another man."

"I don't like knowing I'm a poor substitute for your exwife, either, but there it is." Mortified by her unruly tongue and blaming it on her completely scattered faculties, she raced upstairs and slammed her bedroom door shut. She still felt shaken, but was half-afraid he might try to follow her.

She tore off the nightshirt and her panties and yanked on jeans and a loose shirt followed by the boots. In the bathroom,

she scrubbed her face as if she could wash away the knowl-
edge of what had just occurred, then grabbed her coat again
and made herself go back downstairs.

The kitchen was empty.

It was only a temporary relief, though, as she heard his
voice coming from the living room. She realized he was
talking on his cell phone and grabbing the reprieve with both
hands, she quickly went outside.

The morning air slapped icily against her cheeks as she
jogged across the frozen ground to the barn. But if she were
afraid that Jake would be hard on her heels, she was wrong.
As she slid open the barn door more fully, she snuck a look
back at the house.

She could see him through the mudroom windows, standing there watching. He still had his cell phone at his ear.

She wasn't certain whether to be disappointed or relieved
and was more than a little afraid that disappointment had a
decisive edge.

Mostly, though, she just felt confused. And the best answer
to that had always been her horses, so she ducked into the
refuge of the barn.

She checked Latitude first, finding him looking bright eyed
and eager for more attention. She felt him over, checking for
any signs of fever or swelling and was relieved to find none,
particularly after the long trip he'd endured the day before.
She gave him fresh water and hay, and moved on to Ziggy and
the other horses, turning them out to the fenced land behind
the barn where they could freely graze on the sparse grass
poking through the snow.

The wind yanked at her braid as she unloaded hay in the
feeder, and broke up the ice in the water trough before hauling
out buckets of hot water to add on top. The steam from the
water lasted only a few minutes as it mixed with the colder
water, and she peered up at the lightening sky. It would be a

gray, cloudy day by the looks of it and she wouldn't be surprised if it snowed soon.

Leaving the horses in the pasture, she went back into the barn.

Jake was there.

Ignoring him as well as the heat that jolted readily through her, she gathered up the wheelbarrow and tools to muck out the stalls and set to work on the last one in the row. She was fortunate that she could have performed the chore blindfolded and asleep, because it was painfully distracting knowing that he might as well have made love to her on her kitchen table.

"You're not a substitute for my ex-wife," he finally said, when she'd finished with the first stall and moved on to the next. "When I'm with you, especially when I'm with you, Tiff is the last one I'm thinking about."

She didn't believe him, but she wasn't going to enter into that argument. Hadn't she already embarrassed herself enough?

"You don't have anything to say about that?"

"I've already said more than I should have." Done far more than she should have. She dumped a shovelful of manure into the wheelbarrow she'd pulled close to the stall gate and twisted back around into the stall, switching to the pitchfork to even out the straw bedding.

"You don't believe me."

She straightened, propping her hands on top of the handle. "No." So much for good intentions. Her fingers were sweating around the wooden handle. "I was there when your aunt told you about your ex-wife's accident. I saw your face! You've never been serious about another woman since she left Forrest's Crossing. Everyone in the stables says you're still in love with her, despite what happened between you."

"So that makes it fact?" He looked incredulous. "I don't know what you saw in my face, honey, but I can promise you it wasn't love. That ended pretty damn quick when I caught her in our bed with my best friend. And they weren't exactly looking for me between the sheets. She was screwing Adam when she was married to me." His teeth bared a little. "Why on God's green earth do you think I would want her after that?"

Hearing the rumors about his wife's infidelity was one thing. Hearing the flat statements from Jake's own lips was another.

"I'm sorry," she said huskily. "It must have been terrible for you. What…what she did."

"Yeah, well, save yourself the hankie."

"Are you saying you didn't care?" Her legs felt shaky all over again. "Why did you marry her if not for love?"

"She was pregnant."

She leaned harder on the pitchfork. "I…see."

His lips twisted. "She lost the baby after the 'I do's.' If there ever *was* a baby. The boys didn't come along until a few years later. Skipping her birth control wasn't something she saw fit to share with me."

"You, uh, you didn't want children?"

"I didn't exactly have a choice, did I?" His voice was flat. "They'd barely started kindergarten before she decided there was more to life than pretending to be my loving wife, even if it did come with the financial perks that she *did* love."

Her throat felt so tight, it ached. "I'm sorry, Jake."

"You weren't the one lying to my face."

He turned his head at the sound of Ryan entering the barn, laden with an extension ladder and painting equipment, so he missed the guilt that J.D. feared would be written on her face.

She hastily turned around to finish cleaning out the stall, not even capable of managing the briefest of introductions between the two. Not that it seemed to matter as she heard the two of them tersely exchange names.

"It looks like it's gonna snow," Ryan said to J.D. "I'll see if I can get the old paint scraped off first and start painting when it clears up a little."

"Fine." She didn't look at either of them as she moved the wheelbarrow again. "There's no hurry." She'd been going to wait until spring, after all.

"That thing's a little heavy for her, don't you think?" Ryan's pointed voice was directed at Jake.

She shot her cousin a glare across the barn where he was arranging his tools, but he seemed to delight in remaining oblivious to her annoyance. "I'm managing just fine," she said to the both of them when it looked like Jake was actually going to try to take the wheelbarrow from her, even though she felt *quite* certain that he'd never personally wheeled horse manure anywhere. "But thanks for the offer, Ryan," she added just as pointedly. If he were truly worried about her, he would have taken the load himself.

She almost thought she caught a whisper of a grin on his face as he busied himself with his painting equipment, but she couldn't be certain. And she was much more concerned with Jake than she was with her cousin, anyway.

More specifically, with the fact that she *was* no better than Jake's ex-wife when it came to anything.

Chapter Ten

"He's still there, then?"

J.D. held the phone to her ear as she peered out the kitchen window toward the barn. "Yes, he's still here." The *he* in question was, of course, Jake. And despite J.D.'s belief that he would lose interest in keeping such close tabs on Latitude, after a week, she was beginning to wonder. "Every morning he shows up right after dawn. The man's like *glue!*"

Her sister laughed softly. "Driving you right up a tree, is he?"

"I don't need him looking over my shoulder when it comes to Latitude." Was that his shadow just inside the barn door? She sidestepped a little, still looking out the window, but from a safer, less noticeable angle.

Angeline laughed a little more. "Oh. Definitely, *that's* what's bothering you."

"You're my sister," she grumbled. "You're not supposed to be taking such delight in my misery."

"I'm your sister and I love you but I'm not going to stand

by and pretend you don't have your head in the sand," Angel countered smoothly. "You've got to deal with the matter, J.D., and the sooner the better. How long do you think it's going to be before someone in the family happens to mention the blessed event that's getting closer with every day that passes? You think Jake isn't going to wonder why you didn't happen to mention to him that you're pregnant?"

It *was* him. He strode out of the barn, carrying a bale of hay as easily as if he'd done so every day of his life.

He also didn't so much as glance at the house. At *her*.

She went to the refrigerator, yanking it open to pull out a block of cheese and the sliced ham that her mother had sent home with her the other night after yet another casually offered invitation to dinner.

And, by the way, why didn't she bring along Jake?

She hadn't had a single meal with her family since Jake had arrived in town that hadn't included him.

It was maddening.

She couldn't seem to get away from him no matter what she did. No matter how many times she tried to convince him that she didn't need his assistance to put Latitude through his very gentle paces, he kept showing up at her place at the crack of dawn each morning. He didn't turn down a single invitation that she was convinced had been issued solely to make her insane.

What was worse, she was afraid she was getting used to it.

Used to him. His constant presence. His quiet, wry humor. His intelligence and the sight of his tall, broad-shouldered body looking more and more at home around *her* home.

But he didn't touch her again.

Not an unintentional brush of hands.

Not an abruptly unexpected kiss.

And certainly not…anything…more.

The nights, though, were the hardest.

If she slept, she dreamt of him. And if she didn't sleep, she thought of him.

"Telling him will only make things more complicated," J.D. said to her sister.

"He has a right to know. Your baby has the right to know."

"My baby has the right to grow up knowing he's completely wanted and utterly loved. The same way *we* grew up." There would be birthday celebrations and holidays and school events and Sunday dinners, and always, *always,* there would be plenty of love. Expressed and returned.

"Letting your child and his father know one another doesn't mean that's not going to happen," Angeline countered reasonably. "This isn't a secret you're going to be able to keep for long, J.D. I know you love to be in control, so I'd think you'd rather control the time and place he learns about it."

"I don't love to be in control."

Angeline laughed outright. "Please. You're making my side hurt here."

J.D. made a face at the block of cheddar as she cut off several thin slices to add to the mound of ham she'd sliced. "You're such a help. I'm so glad I called you."

Angeline's laughter calmed. "Can I help it if I think you're making this harder than it has to be? Tell him."

Her sister wasn't telling her anything her own conscience wasn't telling her. "He's made it plain that he doesn't consider himself a family man, Angel."

"Neither did Brody and look at *him.*"

"Brody's head over heels in love with you, and vice versa," J.D. countered. "Jake is not in love with me."

"Are you in love with him?"

She made a mangled mess out of the plastic wrap she snapped off the roll. "I'm thirty-one, Angeline. I know exactly who and what I am, and am just fine with it. And *that* woman is not at all the type that Jake chooses."

"That's not an answer, sister dear."

"I don't do love, remember?" Not well, at any rate. And falling for Jake would be the height of impossibility.

"Oh, for heaven's sake, J.D.! You and Donny were barely out of college," Angeline reminded, sounding exasperated. "That's just old water under an old bridge. And might I also point out that whatever *type* you think is Jake's, he *chose* to sleep with you."

J.D. gave up on the wrap and leaned over to shove it in the trash beneath the sink. "Blame it on the champagne."

When she straightened, Jake was standing in the doorway. "Blame *what* on the champagne?"

She felt the blood drain out of her head and wasn't entirely certain whether to blame *him* or the pregnancy they'd created. "Nothing." She waved at the sandwiches she'd been in the middle of assembling and walked blindly out of the kitchen.

Fortunately, she was already familiar with the layout of her new home and managed not to walk straight into a wall before her vision started to clear.

"J.D.?" Angeline's voice was sharp. "What's wrong?"

"Nothing," she repeated again. "I've got to get lunch on," she said, "before I go into town. I'll talk to you later."

"He's there, isn't he?"

"Yes. Love you, too." She hit the end button, squashing her conscience at the same time.

"Here."

She nearly jumped out of her skin, and looked back to see Jake standing behind her, a sandwich in his extended hand. Why couldn't the man make some noise when he moved? "I made those for you and Ryan."

He didn't lower the sandwich. "And the last time you looked this pale, you about passed out at my dining-room table at Forrest's Crossing. *Eat.*"

She didn't need any reminders of that day at his palatial mansion. She snatched the sandwich and brushed past him back into the kitchen. "I saw you hauling out that fresh hay. You didn't need to." She pulled out a plate and set the second sandwich on it. "Here."

"Didn't it need to be done?"

"Yes, but feeding the horses I board is my responsibility. Not yours."

"Thank you, Jake." His voice was arid. "I appreciate the help."

She just looked at him.

He let out a sigh and yanked out one of the chairs at the small table. "I know that you *know* what graciousness is about. Because I've met your mother." He sat down and picked up his sandwich. "Thank you for the lunch."

She planted her palms on the table and leaned toward him. "Thank you for pulling out the hay. You're welcome for the lunch. Now, why don't you stop playing games and go back to your world?"

He lifted an eyebrow. "My world. Your world. Never realized before what a snob you are, J.D." He sank his white teeth into the thick sandwich.

She straightened and whirled around to the counter, rapidly fixing another sandwich for Ryan, which she wrapped in a napkin and carried out to the mudroom. She opened the door there, wincing a little at the cold air that blew in, and yelled his name. He appeared seconds later, silently took the sandwich and headed back to the barn.

She found herself envying her cousin's antisocial attitude.

Steeling herself, she went back into the kitchen and forced down a few bites of the sandwich while standing next to the counter. "I'll be in town most of this afternoon," she finally said. "Evan will be by later to check on Latitude. There's really no need for you to hang around."

"I'll drive you to town."

"Then I'd just need a ride back home again."

"And that's a problem because…?"

Her fingers curled. "Because you'll have to drive me back again."

"So?"

She exhaled noisily. "So, I want my own truck with me." And she did *not* want him dropping her off in front of the offices of Weaver OB/GYN. "I have errands to run, Jake." She waved her hand restlessly. "Shopping. Girl…stuff."

His lips twitched. "Girl…stuff."

"Is that so hard to believe? I *am* a girl."

"Believe me." His gaze ran down her body, leaving a trail of heat in its wake. "I am well aware of that." He picked up his sandwich again. "But fine. Go do your stuff. I'll wait here."

No reprieve for the wicked.

"There's really nothing for you to do—"

"I want to talk to Evan."

Which just had worry of another sort assaulting her. "Latitude is doing well, Jake."

"And I still want to talk to Evan." He gave her a look. "Just because Latitude is loving all of your attention doesn't mean he's out of the woods, yet."

"I know that."

His gaze was steady. "Do you, really?"

"It's only been a week. If you're worried about laminitis, he's not showing any signs of it." The disease had a number of causes and no respect for class of horse—pleasure or athletic or anything in between—but it could easily strike a horse who was unable to equally distribute his weight on all four feet. While Latitude's broken leg might be healing, another foot could become even more of an issue. Laminitis wasn't just painful. It could become so severe that the hoof separated from the bone. A few of the most famous racehorses of all time had been humanely euthanized when stricken with the excruciating disease.

"And I could name off another half dozen things that could go wrong in addition to laminitis."

"Well, given that his very life is on the line, you can give him more than a week!"

"And I will when I'm convinced he's actually improving."

She pressed her lips together, wanting to argue, but knowing he was entitled to his opinion. And also knowing that he wasn't completely in the wrong. No horse should have to suffer if there was no end to it in sight.

The problem was, they didn't *know* where that "end" was, much less what it might hold. It was too early.

The clock on the oven behind Jake's shoulder indicated that she was already cutting the time close before she was due at the doctor's office. "Rinse your plate and put it in the dishwasher when you're finished," she said, and sped out of the room and up the stairs where she quickly changed into clean jeans and a long-sleeved blouse and hustled back down again, yanking a brush through her hair as she went.

Jake was still at the kitchen table, evidently finishing the rest of the sandwich that she'd abandoned. He had his cell phone at his ear, but told her to drive carefully before she left out the back door.

Outside, she saw Ryan high on the ladder next to the barn. He was still scraping away the peeling paint and he lifted one hand in a sketch of a wave as she climbed in her truck and backed down the drive.

By the time she made it to the doctor's office, her nerves felt so tight she wanted to scream.

Was it any wonder, then, that Dr. Keegan sat J.D. down in her office after she'd examined her and asked her bluntly if she was under any undue stress? "You're obviously tense." The young doctor folded her hands together on top of her desk and looked at J.D. "Is there anything you want to talk about?"

"As long as the baby is healthy, I'm just fine," J.D. assured.

The doctor didn't look convinced. She wrote out a prescription and handed it across the desk. "For your prenatal vitamins," she said. "And I want to see you after Thanksgiving for an ultrasound."

The little square of paper crinkled as J.D.'s fingers tightened. "The baby *is* healthy, right?"

"It appears to be," the doctor said calmly. "But this is our first visit together and you're a little small for seventeen weeks. Since your previous OB didn't order one for you, I'd like to. The ultrasound will give me a better idea of your true due date. Plus, you can find out the sex of the baby, if you want to know."

"It's a boy," she said. "I know it is. And I already gave you the date I conceived."

The doctor smiled. "I know some women think they can pinpoint exactly the moment they conceive, but that's usually more of an emotional response than science. Conception could have occurred even during one of the less momentous of lovemak—"

"There's only *one* moment," J.D. interrupted. And it most certainly had been momentous, and not because she'd had any inkling whatsoever that she and Jake had been creating a new human being. "One man. One time."

The doctor blinked a little. "Oh. I see."

J.D. doubted it. She'd chosen to use Dr. Keegan as her obstetrician because she was filling in for the practice's owner, who was on sabbatical. Most specifically, this doctor wasn't in any way affiliated with J.D.'s family. Much as she loved them, this was one time she'd wanted someone around who was completely objective. "So, there's no question about the calendar," J.D. finished. "And if the baby *is* too small, what does that mean?"

"It may mean nothing," Dr. Keegan assured. "Truly, J.D., don't let this stress you out more than you already are."

"I'm not stressed!"

The other woman just lifted her eyebrows a little. "Would you like me to take your blood pressure right now?"

J.D. realized her hands were clenched over the wooden arms of her chair and subsided. "Okay," she sighed. "Maybe a little."

"Anything you want to talk about?"

"I don't think they taught the answers to my problem in medical school."

"What's the problem?" The other woman's gaze flicked to J.D.'s chart. "Anything to do with the *one* man, *one* time?" Her lips curved gently. "It's not such a stretch, given your condition."

"I thought I was doing the right thing by not telling him." She folded the prescription precisely in half. Then in half, again. "But how can I be sure?"

"Is he a danger to you or the baby?"

Only to their hearts.

She shook her head. "He's not dangerous that way."

The doctor leaned across the desk a little. "Well. The one thing I can tell you is probably what you already know. Bringing a baby into the world is more easily done when there are two parents. Maybe that's not entirely PC anymore, but that's the reality. Babies are an immense amount of work. An incredible responsibility." She smiled slightly. "All worthwhile, of course. At least in my opinion."

J.D. glanced at the framed photograph of a little girl on the credenza behind the doctor. "How old is she?"

The doctor glanced back at the photo. "Chloe's almost seven now." She looked back at J.D. "And I can tell you from experience that being a single parent isn't exactly an easy road, even when you do have a solid support system around you."

"Telling the father isn't going to change my support system," J.D. murmured. She could always count on her family for that.

But from Jake? The baby would get every other tangible thing he could provide. And given his wealth, that wasn't insignificant. But would he provide what counted most?

Love?

She was no closer to an answer for that than she'd ever been. "I appreciate your time, Dr. Keegan." She pushed out of the chair, putting an end to her internal debate.

"That's what I'm here for, J.D. If something's disturbing you, I want to hear about it. Taking care of mom isn't just about vitamins and blood tests." Dr. Keegan rose, too, and walked with J.D. out to the reception area. She set J.D.'s chart on the counter. "Don't forget to set that appointment."

"I won't."

The woman smiled again and turned to the other patient in the waiting area. The two disappeared behind the door again. J.D. made her appointment, paid the fee for the office visit, and walked down the street to the corner drug store where she filled the prescription. It was the same thing that the doctor in Atlanta had prescribed and she tossed the bottle in her purse and drove back through town, stopping in at Classic Charms, the quaint shop that Tara owned and operated. Her cousin-in-law wasn't in the shop that afternoon, but J.D. still enjoyed browsing the eclectic selection. Since Tara had married Axel and had Aidan, she'd begun carrying a fair-sized collection of baby items and J.D. felt drawn to it.

Tiny little jeans. Macho little sweatshirts. Frilly dresses that seemed so small nothing human could possibly fit into them.

She picked up a knitted sweater in a bright blue and felt such a squeeze of yearning inside her that her eyes went damp. What a mess she was.

But she simply couldn't make herself put the sweater back and when she left the store, the sweater was nestled in tissue at the bottom of one of the store's pretty shopping bags.

The sun was angling lower in the sky that had gotten

heavier and grayer since she'd driven to town. A few snow-flakes drifted in the air and she flipped her collar up more closely around her neck as she hurried the few blocks back to her car.

By the time she made it home, it was snowing in earnest. She left the shopping bag in the mudroom and went out to the barn. Jake was there, along with Ryan, nearly finished with settling the horses inside for the night.

"It's starting to come down pretty hard," she warned as she joined them. "If you want to get back to town, you'd better go now."

Typically, neither man seemed bent on listening to her and she mentally tossed her hands in the air and asked Jake instead how Evan's visit with Latitude had gone.

"He's satisfied the break is beginning to heal, finally."

The relief that shot through her was wide and sweeping and she practically threw her arms around Latitude's satiny neck. "You hear that? You're healing!" She was still grinning when she faced Jake again. It was all she could do not to hug *him,* too, but the odd expression on his face kept her in line. "What?"

He shook his head a little. "Just haven't seen you smile like that in a while." His voice dropped a notch and he grazed a lock of hair trailing over her shoulder with his fingertip. "It's good to see."

Which had her emotions clutching at something nameless just as surely as they had in Tara's shop.

"Damn it, Bonneville," Ryan's annoyed voice broke the spell and she looked over to see him pushing aside the horse. "Somebody ought to bite you back," he groused as he slammed the stall gate shut.

Jake's hand fell away from J.D.'s hair and they quickly finished bedding down the animals before heading back to the warmth of the house.

J.D. didn't want to let herself think about just how cozy it all felt.

She threw together a quick dinner of biscuits and beef stew and the snow just came down harder. "Decide between you who gets the guest room and who gets the couch," she told them as she was washing up afterward.

Despite her efforts at nonchalance, her gaze caught on Jake's and she quickly looked back at the sudsy water in the sink. "There's a packing box in the mudroom still that has extra sheets and blankets." She still had things she was unpacking and at that particular moment, she was glad that she hadn't gotten to the point of decorating the extra bedroom as a nursery.

In the reflection of the window above the sink, she saw Ryan push away from the table and go into the mudroom. He came back with a stack of bedding from the box, as well as the bag from Classic Charms, which he dropped on the kitchen table. "Don't think there's a woman in our family who can go by Tara's shop without buying something," he said with faint humor before disappearing down the hall.

Jake glanced inside the bag. "What'd you get?"

She practically snatched the bag out of his hands. "Nothing."

His eyebrow peaked. "What are you afraid of? That I'll see you bought some frilly piece of lingerie or something?"

"I don't do frilly," she said witheringly.

A glint came into his eyes that had heat blasting through her. "I remember exactly what you *do*."

She clutched the bag to her chest and tore out of the room like the hounds of hell were at her heels. It didn't help at all that the sound of Jake's low laughter trailed her only by a nose.

Chapter Eleven

The snow lasted for three days.

Which meant, essentially, that J.D. had houseguests for three days.

Ryan was no bother. He kept himself practically invisible unless he was sitting at the table eating with her and Jake. She found herself wishing her cousin would be around a little more often, because she could have used an extra buffer against Jake's proximity.

Her only escape from the disturbing man was when she'd exercise and groom the horses because that's usually when Jake disappeared with his computer and cell phone, taking care of what Forco business that his sister, Charlotte, couldn't.

By the time the snow stopped and the roads were cleared for more than an hour at a time, and both of her houseguests could return to their usual non-luxurious digs at the Sleep Tite, J.D. was pathetically grateful for the reprieve.

Only as proof of her contrary emotions, instead of sleeping

better at night knowing that Jake wasn't just a few feet away in the room next to hers, she felt his absence even more acutely.

By the time the afternoon before Thanksgiving rolled around, she was about ready to come out of her skin.

The following day, the family would have a huge, traditional meal at the Double-C, which was pretty much the only place left where their sheer numbers could still comfortably gather together inside. Plus, it gave her grandfather—who still lived there along with Gloria, even though the massive ranch was really run now by his son, Matthew—a chance to wear his patriarch hat, which was something the cantankerous old man loved doing.

J.D.'s contribution to the inevitable feast was the four apple pies she'd made from scratch that were sitting on the counter in the kitchen. She'd had plenty of time to make them, wandering around her very empty house in the middle of the night while peaceful sleep eluded her.

She'd mucked out the stalls, the horses were groomed, and restlessness plagued her. She could have gone into the house to take care of her bookkeeping—it was time to send out her invoices—but sitting at a desk held zero appeal. Plus, Jake was inside, working at the kitchen table in what he had sort of turned into his office away from home.

Restlessness plaguing her, she went out to the corral and whistled for Ziggy. He and Latitude both trotted over and J.D. let Ziggy out of the gate, holding back an eager Latitude. "Sorry, handsome," she told him, scrubbing her hand down his neck. "Not this time."

He huffed out a breath and hung his head over the fence, watching as she saddled up Ziggy. But when Bonneville trotted past him, he jerked his head around and jogged after the other horse. Even with his leg screwed together in a cast, Lat wanted to compete.

The fact that he did was just more proof of the young horse's incredible will.

J.D. swung up onto Ziggy and rode him over to the back of the house and knocked on the kitchen window.

All she intended to do was let Jake know that she was going out for a short ride.

But when he came over to the window to look out at her, the words to emerge weren't at all that simple. "Want to go for a ride?" She spoke loud enough to be heard through the window.

He drew his brows drew together. "What?"

Ziggy shifted beneath her. He was clearly anxious to get moving and standing next to the house while she peered up into the kitchen window wasn't exactly what he had in mind. "Or has it been so long you don't remember how to ride?"

"I remember."

She pulled Ziggy around into a tight circle, still eyeing Jake. "Well?"

His gaze narrowed. "I'm not riding that godforsaken Bonneville," he said. "Damn horse tried to take a bite out of my jacket yesterday."

It wasn't a flat-out "no," and she was appalled at the giddiness that fluttered through her stomach. "You can take Ziggy, here. I'll run out Hepburn." The mare was one of her boarders and a sweet one to exercise.

When he gave a short nod and moved away from the window, her giddiness quadrupled.

She clucked to Ziggy and he headed reluctantly back to the barn. She was nearly finished saddling Hepburn when Jake joined her. He'd pulled on his shearling coat and leather gloves, but left his head bare. And she just felt uncommonly nervous. "I have several English saddles if you prefer one."

"This is fine."

"You've ridden western before?"

His eyes crinkled a little. "Is that so hard to believe?"

She flipped down the stirrup and gathered Hepburn's reins. "It's not quite what I expected." There were a lot of things about Jake that weren't quite what she expected. And it was causing her some consternation. "We won't go far," she said, leading Hepburn out of the barn and keeping a weather eye out on Jake with Ziggy. "Do you want a leg up?"

"I haven't ridden since the dark ages, but I think I can handle it." His voice was even drier. "Do you?"

In answer, she smoothly swung up into the saddle. And darned if she didn't have to swallow a little harder at the sight of Jake easily doing the same. "In all the years I've known you, I've never seen you astride a horse."

"And watching you ride in the mornings at Forrest's Crossing was one of the best parts of my day," he returned blandly. "Where're we headed?"

Thoroughly sidetracked by the disturbing notion that he'd watched her at all, she aimed toward the open field beyond the riding arena. They still had a few hours of strong light left, and the sun felt good and warm against the crisp air.

They rode in silence for quite a while though J.D. kept sneaking looks at Jake's face. His thoughts looked like they were elsewhere, though, so she was surprised when he was the one to break the silence. "Is this still your property?"

"I wish." She pointed toward a line of trees they'd passed a while back. "That shelter belt there is the property line. Now we're on Johnny Hanks' land." She looked across the acreage. "He's trying to sell. I thought about buying it instead of my place. It's a great piece of land. But the house needed more work than I had time—than I wanted to deal with," she amended quickly. And selfishly, she hoped the spread would still be available when she was able to afford it.

"What's so great about it?"

She lifted her shoulder. "There's water, for one thing.

Stream runs across about a third of the way back. It's good grazing. Could have a lot of horses out here."

"Thought you said you were finished with racing."

"I am. But there's plenty of other training I can do. And—" She broke off.

His gaze sharpened on her face. "And, what?"

"Well, *you're* going to think it's a waste, probably, but I've been thinking about starting up a horse rescue operation someday."

His lips tightened. "Hell of an opinion you must have of me, J.D. What do you think I want to do? Send every nag off to the glue factory?"

"No!" She wished she'd kept her mouth shut. "I'm sorry. That just didn't come out right. I only meant that I know your interest in horses is more...less..." She let out a breath. No matter what she tried to say, it was going to come out wrong.

"I'm in it for the money?"

"Aren't you?"

"Horseracing is in the Forrest blood," he said. "My grandfather. My father. Me."

"That's why you want the Derby so badly? To follow in their footsteps?"

"That's the only remaining difference between my father and me."

She studied him for a moment. "You don't look particularly happy. Is it the difference or the similarities that are so objectionable?"

"There you go again, looking for stuff that's not there."

"And there you go again with the cynicism. I know, I know." She waved a hand before he could comment. "Because you are your father's son."

"Can't deny blood."

She looked away. Wasn't she guilty of thinking the same

thing about herself? She cleared her throat. Shifted in the saddle and earned a look from Hepburn. "How else are you like him?"

"Named for him. Look like him. Have all of his best—" his voice implied something much less positive "—traits. My sons hate me just like I hated him."

Her heart squeezed. "You are so wrong about that, Jake." She'd seen for herself just the opposite. "Zach and Connor don't hate you."

He frowned. "Ask 'em."

"Maybe I would," she returned rapidly, "if they were around to ask. Then you could see that I'm right. Zach and Connor need a father, Jake. They need you."

"The father that mattered to them was Adam."

"And he's gone. Their mother is still convalescing and will be for months. They're grieving and they need to know that you *are* their father and that it's okay for them to have loved you both!"

"That implies that they've ever loved me."

"Have you even let them know you?" She leaned toward him, rocking slightly with the horse's plodding steps. "How often did you go visit them once you and Tiffany split up? Once a year? Twice?" She'd be willing to bet money that it hadn't been more often than that. And she knew for a fact how many times they'd been to Forrest's Crossing since then. Once. And that was when Jake had brought them back after the car accident. "How *could* they know you when you've intentionally kept yourself out of their lives?"

He just shook his head as if she were suggesting pure nonsense and lifted his hand, pointing into the distance. "Is that the creek over there?"

She nodded.

"Bet I can beat you there." He didn't wait for her answer, but launched Ziggy off across the smooth field.

Disconcerted by his abruptness, it took a second before J.D. sent Hepburn after them.

If she'd had any worries that Jake was out of practice on horseback, they were quickly banished.

The man rode beautifully. Expertly.

And she focused a little harder as adrenaline started gathering inside her. Hepburn was younger than Ziggy though not as naturally speedy, but carrying Jake, who was considerably larger and heavier than J.D., left them well matched. A competitive spark shot through her veins, particularly when Hepburn edged alongside Ziggy and Jake sent her a sideways look.

"Don't be so sure," she called, bending low over Hepburn's neck, urging her faster. Neither Ziggy nor Jake were going to be outdone, though, and they traded the inch-lead back and forth as chunks of snow kicked up from beneath pounding hooves. By the time J.D. reined in Hepburn just seconds behind Ziggy, she was laughing breathlessly. "You're a hustler," she accused as he dismounted.

"Credit the horse." Before she could protest, he'd lifted her right off of Hepburn and set her on the ground. His gaze seemed to focus on her lips, and her heart was suddenly racing for a brand new reason. "And yes, I like to win. Just like my old man." He slid his finger beneath a lock of hair straying across her cheek, slowly twirling along the curl.

Her lips seemed to tingle. She wanted his kiss so badly she could taste it. And because she did, she made herself move away.

It took every bit of strength she possessed.

She ducked around Jake's wide shoulder and gathered up Hepburn's and Ziggy's reins, walking them to a well-graveled curve in the creek bed that allowed easier access to the flowing water. Despite the cold temperature, both horses drank eagerly.

J.D. turned her face up to the warm sun and unzipped her coat.

"Little different than a humid night in Georgia." Jake stopped next to her. He'd not only undone his coat, but shrugged right out of it. He rolled it up and fastened it to Ziggy's saddle. "Can't believe it feels this warm, though. Just a few days ago, it was pretty much a blizzard."

Did he think it would be so easy to go back to discussing something so inconsequential as the weather? "That's the way it is sometimes. Growing up, the schools would close for a snow day, then a week later, we'd practically be begging our parents to let us go out to the swimming hole at the C." She shook her head, remembering. "I think there were times when we went swimming that we had ice crystals on our skin. I loved growing up here. We didn't even have to work hard for friends when there was a bunch built in thanks to all the cousins Angel and I have."

"Lucky you."

"Why'd you hate your father?"

He let out a sigh. Resigned. "He was a bastard who used up anyone and everyone who ever tried to love him. I wish he'd never existed."

"And if he hadn't, neither would you or your sisters. Or your sons. Do you wish that, too?"

He grimaced. "Obviously, that was an expression."

"What about your mother?"

"Once she and the old man were finished playing tug-of-war for me and my sisters, she left with a fortune in her pocket and no desire to come back."

"But they both wanted you, then."

"No." He gave her a pitying look. "They wanted to be in control of the money my grandmother had put in trust for us. Grandmother Deveraux was the old money. She married Grandfather Forrest who was the new."

"And what about your aunt Susan? She helped raise you, didn't she? Or are you going to try to tell me that was about *the money*, too?"

"Susan stayed loyal to Jacob Forrest because she loved him. Period."

"Your mother's sister was in love with your father?"

"She centered her life around us after my mother walked out. She never married. Never had children of her own. And yeah, she filled in the gaps of raising us that good old Olivia and Jacob left. She loved him. It's the only explanation."

"Does it occur to you that she loved *you* and your sisters?" She stared at him. "Why do you find it so difficult to believe someone might love you? Just because of *you?*"

"Because no one ever has." His voice was matter-of-fact. "Not even the ones who should have. And you can stop letting this put a frown on your face. It's all water under the bridge."

"Not when it's affecting the relationship you have with your children." Even the one he didn't know about.

His lips tightened. "If it was so great for you growing up here, why'd you move away in the first place?"

"Went to college. Fell in love." She tucked her fingertips in the front pockets of her jeans.

"What happened?"

She bit the inside of her lip and stared across the stream. "I cheated on him," she admitted bluntly. She looked at him, her shoulders tight. "Shocked?"

"At what's undoubtedly your very worst secret?" Sunlight cast across his face, illuminating the clear brown of his eyes. "You weren't in love with him."

"What makes you so sure of that?" Though he was right. And she could finally recognize it now, because she *was* in love with Jake. The realization came with no blinding force. Just a certainty that was all the more powerful because of its very simplicity.

"Because I know you. You're the most straightforward person I know."

She looked away. "No. I'm really not."

Tell him.

The words circled inside her head and her throat started aching. How could she love him, but remain silent?

"I envy you that, actually."

She shot him an incredulous look. "Sorry?"

"You know what it is you want and don't want and you live your life accordingly."

"I understand you have obligations with Forco. But you also own some of the finest horses in the world. You live in a mansion straight out of *Gone with the Wind*. You have the money to do just about anything you want, anywhere. So, how are you *not* living your life the way you want?"

"I took over Forco because I had to when my father died." He stepped over to Ziggy again and ran his hand along the horse's long neck. "Not because I wanted to."

She stared at the sharp, clean lines of his profile. "What would you rather have done?"

The corner of his mouth hitched up a notch. "Farm, if you can believe it."

Her lips parted a little; the image so different than anything she could have expected. "Farm…what?"

"Whatever. Anything." He rolled his shoulders. "I was studying agribusiness in college when my father died. It was either step in and take the reins or let the company fall to someone who *wasn't* a Forrest." He glanced over at her. "Which is not done in my family."

"You're very good at it, considering. The company's done nothing but grow under your leadership."

"Training racehorses is something you excelled at, but you say that's not what you really loved doing. You just love horses. Period."

"Yes." She pressed her lips together for a moment. "So…would you still want to be a farmer?"

He rolled his shoulders, not seeming to notice the diffidence in her question. "And end up a pauper? No, thanks." He paused a moment. "I'm not ignorant of the perks of my position. I'm well aware of the advantages I've had and use them all to my convenience whenever it suits me. And that's not something I'm willing to give up anymore. But my life isn't anything I'd wish on someone else."

She had no business feeling disappointment. She was supposed to have her eyes open where Jake was concerned. "Like who? The sons you are *so* wrong about?"

"Zach and Con will be nothing like me," he said flatly. "I'm making certain of it."

"How? By letting them think you don't want anything to do with them?" She huffed out a breath. "You know what was the best thing about being raised here?"

"I'm sure you're going to tell me."

"Straightforward," she reminded tartly. "The best thing my parents gave me was *time*. Their time. And not just them. All of the family. We all grew up knowing we were wanted. Loved. And not because they *told* us. Which they did. But because they showed us. Day in and day out. And…and that's what I want to give my children." She nearly choked, getting the words past the knots inside her chest and throat.

"Exactly what I don't give mine," he said. "That's what you really mean."

"It doesn't matter what I mean," she said, frustrated. "It *matters* what you do! I'm sorry you hated your father. I really am. But you are not him. Are you going to live your entire life—go to *your* grave—knowing that when you had an opportunity to be different than him, you ignored it?"

But his expression was clearly set, and she shivered, yanking the zipper up on her coat. "It's getting cold again." In more ways than one.

He immediately drew Ziggy's reins out of her loose grip. "Then it's time to get back."

She couldn't look at him, afraid if she did, the tears lodged behind her eyes would break loose. She swung up into the saddle and turned Hepburn away from the creek.

This time when they rode, there was no racing. No laughter.

Only silence.

Chapter Twelve

"Happy Thanksgiving!"

J.D. stared stupidly at the blonde woman standing on her front porch. What was Jake's aunt doing there?

"I know it's unexpected," Susan went on, as if her presence really wasn't unexpected at all. "But Jake wasn't at the hotel when we stopped by there first."

"We?"

Susan waved toward the fancy SUV parked behind J.D.'s truck alongside the house, and J.D. was even more disconcerted to see Zach and Connor hopping out of the vehicle.

She blinked a little. The sky above was clear as a bell. She could smell the wood smoldering in her fireplace. Could feel the cold air touching her face.

She wasn't dreaming.

"I'm sorry, but Jake's not here," she said faintly. After they'd put up the horses following their ride yesterday, he'd gathered his computer and cell phone from her kitchen table and left.

And that morning, for the first time since he'd come to Wyoming, he hadn't been at the barn ready to greet her when she went out to tend the horses.

She'd done the chores on her own. Alone. And had known that his absence wasn't owed to some observance of the holiday. It was owed to her *straightforward* comments.

The boys' feet pounded on the steps as they reached them. "I gotta pee," Connor greeted, brushing right past her into the house.

She pointed down the hallway. "On the right."

He hustled through the living room and Zach followed more slowly. His eyes, so like his father's, took her in from head to toe. "You look different," he said.

She was *not* going to feel guilty in front of a nine-year-old. She brushed at the long hem of her oversize flannel shirt while the outdoor breeze blew through the open door, sharp and cold. "Is that good or bad?"

He cocked his head to one side, again eerily echoing one of Jake's mannerisms. "Good," he finally decided. "Connor thinks you're real pretty."

She bit the inside of her lip. "Tell him I said thank you." J.D. looked above him to Jake's aunt, pulling the door wider. "Come in."

"Thanks." Susan's cheeks were rosy.

J.D. pushed the door closed after her. "I'm sorry to seem a little dim, but I'm so surprised to see you."

"Well, that makes us all surprised then," Susan said with a wry smile. "And no need to apologize, dear. We're the ones barging in on you. And on Thanksgiving Day, yet." She started to unwind a narrow lilac scarf from around her neck. "Lord, but it's cold. Jake warned me to come prepared, but truly, I had no idea!"

"Jake…warned you? He knows you're here?"

"Of course." Susan's gaze settled on J.D. "Obviously, he didn't tell you we were coming."

"No," she said quietly.

"Well, he did just make the arrangements yesterday," Susan allowed, oblivious to the shock she sent sweeping through J.D. "And I assumed we'd find him here when he wasn't at that quaint little hotel. Everything in town looked like it was closed up for the holiday and he didn't answer his cell phone."

Her knees felt unsteady and she sank down on the arm of the couch. "The cell service around here can be spotty at times."

"That must be it, then." Susan was looking around the living room, curiosity bright in her eyes. "You know, I've traveled all over the world, but this is the very first time I've been to Wyoming."

J.D. was still trying to comprehend the fact that Jake's aunt and sons were there at all. And that Jake, evidently, was the one to initiate it.

Had her words had some effect, after all?

"I don't expect to see Jake until later today. He was, um, going to join my family for dinner."

She couldn't hazard a guess what his intentions were now.

"Turkey?"

She looked over at Connor, coming back into the room. Hunger was plain on his face. "Turkey. Ham. Beef." With that crowd, there was always an assortment.

"We were gonna have sushi in California," Zach informed.

J.D. withheld a shudder. She wasn't a big fan on a good day. Add in her pregnancy-induced finicky senses, and it sounded even less appealing to her.

Susan pulled out her cell phone and began punching numbers. She held the phone to her ear, then a moment later sighed and tucked the phone away again. "Just his voice mail. I wonder where he could be?"

Since she had no clue, J.D. could only shake her head.

Susan eyed the boys. "Why don't you two go outside and look around. I'm sure J.D. won't mind."

She eagerly focused on something her addled brains could comprehend. "Go ahead. The horses are all in the small corral next to the barn. Even Latitude. Just be sure not to open any gates."

"How *is* Latitude doing?" Susan asked when Zach threw open the door, Connor hard on his heels.

"Better." J.D. watched the two scurry down the porch steps, pulling on their coats again as they went, and closed the door once more. "My cousin's husband is a vet. He's been working with him. The break is definitely healing and Latitude is clearly moving better. Even running some."

"Thank heavens for that." Susan shrugged out of her coat and dropped it on the couch beside her. "I'll confess that I'm surprised my nephew has spent as much time here as he has." Her gaze was speculative. "He doesn't even spend this much time in a single stretch at Forrest's Crossing."

J.D. felt her face heat. "He's quite involved with Latitude's rehab."

"Indeed," Susan murmured, a hint of amusement on her face.

"I don't know where my manners are. Can I get you something warm to drink?"

"Coffee would be heavenly."

"Coming right up." She quickly headed back toward the kitchen. But Jake's aunt followed.

"I find the landscape here intriguing. Jake told me I would and he was right. I photograph babies, but when I look out at all that snow, I want to reach for my camera."

"I think it's pretty beautiful." J.D. pulled down a mug and filled it with coffee from the needless pot she'd made, considering Jake's absence that morning. She turned to hand the mug to the other woman when the kitchen door opened, and Jake strode in looking as if he did so every day.

Which until that morning, he basically did.

And J.D. also couldn't help the relieved leap inside her

chest, though he barely glanced at her as he went to his aunt, dropping a kiss on her cheek.

"Trip go okay?" He was clearly unsurprised that she was there, in J.D.'s kitchen.

"As okay as it can go with those boys," Susan returned. "And happy Thanksgiving, darling. Zach and Connor are outside, hopefully not doing too much damage to anything. Where were you? We went by the motel before we came here."

"I was looking at a property with Ryan."

"Ryan!" J.D. started with even more surprise. "What property?"

"The Hanks' place."

Maybe she was having some weird dream and none of this was real at all. "Ryan's interested in buying it?" Could her cousin be feeling so much more comfortable again in Weaver that he was considering buying the very spread she had her eye on?

"I'm interested in it."

Shock held her still as she stared at Jake. "Since when?" She'd only mentioned the place yesterday. "And for what?"

They all heard the clatter on the porch steps a moment before the door flew open and Jake's sons burst in.

"Latitude looks great!" The animation on Zach's face dried up entirely at the sight of his father standing in the middle of the kitchen. "Oh."

"Hello, Zach. Connor."

J.D. wanted badly for Jake to show them some affection. To hug his boys. To make the first move and show he was glad he'd brought them there.

But he did nothing. And she couldn't take the pained expressions on the boys' faces a moment longer. "Hey, guys. Want to help me bring in the horses for the afternoon?" She'd be spending practically the rest of the day at the Double-C. Which meant she needed to stable the horses before she left.

And the sooner she could leave, the better, because she

didn't know what to make of Jake's actions and her foolish emotions were getting way too far ahead of themselves.

The boys looked relieved and trotted after her as she pulled on her coat and went outside.

"How come the horses don't freeze?" Connor asked, skipping to keep up with her.

"They could if they didn't have adequate food to eat and enough weight on them. But they're inside at night when it's coldest, and when they're outside, it's not as cold to them as it feels to you." She pulled open the gate to the corral where the horses were grazing. "Hold this for me, would you?"

The boys eagerly wrapped their hands around the wood.

Ziggy immediately came trotting over at her sharp whistle, followed quickly by Hepburn and Tracy. She slipped on halters and lead ropes and led them out of the corral, telling the boys to push the gate closed. Then, even though Ziggy didn't really need a lead, she handed his rope to Zach. "Bring him into the barn."

Connor looked disappointed, but she put him in charge of closing the stall gates, which seemed to mollify him. And then they all went back out to the corral once more and she whistled again, hiding a smile at the efforts both boys gave at mimicking her.

Latitude's head swiveled in her direction, but it was obvious that he was darned content right where he was alongside Bonneville, who ignored her altogether. Lat swished his long black tail as if to say "don't bug me" and lowered his head to yank at a tuft of stubborn grass peeking up above the snow.

She let his spurt of contrary independence slide and pulled in two more horses, letting Zach and Connor each take a lead this time, and once the horses were stalled, headed back out yet again. She slipped into the corral, heading toward the running buddies.

Jake had left the house and was crossing toward her. He wasn't wearing a coat, and the ever-present breeze was rippling his white shirt against his torso.

She let out a careful breath, not quite able to tear her gaze from him as she ran her hand along Bonneville's neck before slipping on his halter.

He turned his head and caught the shoulder of her coat in his teeth.

She jerked away, feeling the fabric of her coat tear in the process and she pulled down on his lead to remind him who was boss. "Cut it out, Bonny." That's what she got for not paying her usual attention.

Jake practically vaulted the fence, running toward them. "Are you all right?" He grabbed her other shoulder, pulling her around so he could see the tear that Bonneville had made. He prodded through the layers like he was looking for torn and bleeding flesh.

"I'm fine." She directed the mischievous horse in a tight circle until he was accompanying her and not the other way around. "Why are you interested in the Hanks' place?" So much for keeping her tongue under control.

"Because you said that you wanted it."

Her heart skittered around and there didn't seem to be a darned thing she could do about it. Bonneville suddenly planted his feet, resisting her altogether. She shortened her hold on the lead, tapping his hip with her other hand. His muscles bunched, but his hindquarters finally shifted and he dropped his head and started forward, only to flatten his ears at the sight of Jake. "Watch it," J.D. started to warn, but Bonneville snapped at him, narrowly missing his arm.

She wasn't one to strike a horse, but she gave him a smart little whack on the nose. *"No."*

"He's a menace." Jake moved a safer distance away.

"He's learned some bad habits," J.D. defended. "Thanks to

owners who didn't care." She prodded Bonneville forward again. "When did you decide to have your aunt bring the boys here?"

"When do you think?"

Her mouth went dry and she made the mistake of lightening her grip on Bonneville's lead and the horse yanked his head free, his powerful body launching toward the open gate. Worse than that, though, was the blur of motion that was Latitude, who saw nothing more than another opportunity to play with his running mate.

She didn't think.

She just moved fast, cutting across Latitude's path, waving her arms and calling him. Anything to divert him from getting out of the gate where there'd be no stopping him from over-taxing his healing leg.

Jake ran too, doing the same thing. The colt suddenly stopped short, pivoting around to avoid them and trotted in the other direction. J.D. was left to chase after Bonneville who'd cleared the gate and was standing as cocky as he could be near the vehicles parked in her gravel drive.

As long as she didn't move toward him, he seemed content to remain still.

Jake had Latitude under control. Shaken even more by Jake's behavior than her own carelessness, she went into the barn, warning the boys to stay where they were and grabbed her lasso before slipping bareback onto Ziggy. She wasn't taking any chances. If Bonneville decided to really run, the only way she'd catch him was on horseback.

Ziggy trotted out of the barn and J.D. gave Bonneville a wide berth, not wanting to spook him any more than he already was. She headed almost directly away from him before circling around to come up on him from the opposite direc-tion. Now if he bolted away from her, he'd likely head toward the barn or the corrals and the open field rather than the road.

She had it all covered.

Except for the one ingredient provided by two nine-year-old Jake Forrest-miniatures when they decided to run across the yard from the barn to the house. "Hold it," J.D. called out in warning.

But it was too late.

Bonneville hadn't taken kindly to their charge, and ran directly toward J.D. and Ziggy. It wasn't the direction she'd expected, but her mount expertly wheeled around as she sent the lasso sailing through the air to settle neatly around Bonneville's neck.

She snugged it up and Bonneville huffed, trotting back around until he eventually stopped, though every muscle in his powerful body strained, keeping the rope tight between them.

"Whoa." She heard one of the boys breathe. "Cool."

She glanced quickly at the boys. "Just remember this moment for the *next* time I tell you to stay put."

Two pairs of wide brown eyes looked at her with fresh respect and she barely kept herself from smiling.

Instead, she focused again on Bonneville. Clucking softly, she urged Ziggy slowly toward the recalcitrant horse while she pulled up the slack in the rope just enough to keep Bonneville mindful, but not enough to make him even more resistant. He was a 1200-pound horse. Cooperation was going to beat out force every day of the week. The horse skittered sideways, clearly unhappy with the lasso, but he was at least skittering in the direction of the barn.

"No amount of money can be worth working with that pain-in-the-ass horse," Jake said when she and Ziggy came even with him as they steadily maneuvered Bonneville into a more agreeable frame of mind. Jake was still inside the corral. Latitude stood quietly alongside him as if he'd been the only innocent party in this particular game.

"It's not about money." She squeezed her legs, clucking to Ziggy and the horse smoothly closed in again on Bonneville.

But the other horse wasn't finished with his arsenal of bad habits and he kicked out at Ziggy, who naturally stopped short, his big body tensing as he let out a warning squeal.

J.D. gave the rope more play and directed Ziggy to back away. "Come on, guys. Play nice now."

His ears flat, Bonneville kicked out again and Ziggy practically bounced sideways, his long neck arching as he bared his teeth toward the younger horse. As far as Ziggy was concerned, *he* was the boss of the place and wasn't about to let some upstart like Bonneville take his spot.

But still, Bonneville didn't back down.

From the corner of her eye, she saw movement and threw out her hand, warning the boys again to stay back. But that left her only holding on to the lasso and when Bonneville reared up, so did the furious Ziggy.

J.D. had no time to control her dismount. From some portion of her mind, she heard Jake shout, then all she could think of was protecting the baby as she curled herself into a ball.

The impact sent the breath right out of her.

Stars exploded inside her head as she blinked, trying to haul in a breath that wouldn't come.

"Don't move." Jake's voice came above her.

Her struggling lungs finally expanded with wind. The first words she croaked were, "Don't let Bonneville run."

"Forget Bonneville." His hands raced over her arms. Her legs. "Are you hurt?"

"I can't forget Bonneville. He's in my care. I'm responsible for him."

Jake let out a string of colorful words and disappeared for a moment.

She closed her eyes, hugging her arms around her middle. *Please, please be all right.*

She heard Jake cursing both horses and tried to sit up, but

a sharp pain shot out from her shoulder and she groaned, subsiding again.

The boys were yelling and soon, Susan was kneeling beside J.D., too. "Good heavens." She bunched up her soft scarf and slid it beneath J.D.'s head. "You poor dear."

"Jake—is he all right?" She craned her head around to see if he was managing. "He's not used to this side of horses."

"Don't be ridiculous," Susan shushed. "The boy grew up around horses. It was the only place he and his father could ever find some semblance of agreeable ground."

She tried to sit up again, this time using her other arm for leverage. She inhaled sharply at the pain that ripped along her collarbone.

Susan's hands gently nudged her down again. "Stay still. Let him handle it."

"Where are the boys?"

"I sent them back into the house. Don't worry."

But she couldn't help it. She was worried.

About Jake and his family. About Latitude. About that darned, bad-mannered Bonneville. And most of all, about the baby. And what Jake would do when he learned what she'd kept from him.

Her hands closed protectively over her stomach and she closed her eyes again. If she stayed very, very still, the pain in her shoulder didn't seem so hideous.

It seemed forever before Jake returned, but in reality she knew it was probably only minutes. "All right." He knelt beside her once again. "That beast is in the corral. Maybe a few more hours out in the cold'll settle him down."

She tried moving again, to see around his broad shoulder to the corral. "Where's Latitude?"

"In the barn along with Ziggy."

She felt some relief at that. Her gaze ran over Jake. His white shirt was smudged with dirt and his fine, wool trousers were covered with dust and snow. "You need a coat," she said stupidly.

He huffed out a short, unamused laugh. "I'm probably feeling better than you or you'd be on your feet already. Where's it hurt?" He shoved aside her coat, his hands skimming alongside her hips.

God. She tried brushing away his hands but it was no use. "It's not the first time I've fallen off a horse." Tears leaked from the corners of her eyes. "It's just the first time I've done so while pregnant," she finished hoarsely.

Chapter Thirteen

Admitting it was almost a relief.

Except Jake's slashing eyebrows pulled fiercely together as he stared at her as if he didn't even recognize her. "You're pregnant?"

"Almost eighteen weeks."

He went deadly still and all she could hear was her pulse pounding in her ears, seeming to tick off every…single… second.

But he didn't shout at her. Didn't curse her. Didn't voice even so much as a question.

He didn't need to. The betrayal he felt was naked on his face as he shoved his arms beneath her and lifted her right off the ground. "Susan," he barked. "Get my coat from inside. My keys are in the pocket."

Obviously shocked, the older woman pushed to her feet and ran to the house.

"Jake—"

"Quiet. You need to see a doctor."

If she hadn't been shaking from head to toe with the reaction that was setting in, she might have bristled. But he was right. She needed to see a doctor.

She turned her face into his shoulder, afraid to even let herself think that the baby could have been harmed.

Surely, God wouldn't give her this miracle, only to snatch it away now? Or maybe that was her punishment for not being truthful with Jake from the very beginning.

"Zach." She could feel his voice rumbling through his chest. "Open the truck door for me."

"Is she gonna be all right?" The boy was carrying Jake's coat and he raced around them, pulling open the truck door.

"We're going to find that out." Jake set her inside on the seat and tucked her coat in before fastening the seatbelt around her.

J.D. caught a glimpse of Zach's white face before Jake closed the door between them.

"Are you gonna take her to the hospital?" The boy trotted after Jake as he rounded the truck.

"Yeah." He yanked open the door and seemed to hesitate as he looked back at his son.

Then he reached out and brushed his hand over Zach's tumbled hair. "This is nothing like your mom, Zach. Everything will be okay. I promise."

The boy's expression was torn. He wanted to trust but it so obviously went against his grain to do so.

A rolling wave of nausea made her close her eyes, though, and a second later, Jake was inside the truck, gunning the engine. The tires crunched over snow. Gravel. Then the smoother, faster highway.

Her shoulder felt like it was on fire.

"Why didn't you tell me?"

She moistened her lips. "I tried."

He was silent, his disbelief a tangible thing.

"That's what I wanted to meet with you about when I came up to the house that time. I was going to tell you then, but Susan interrupted us."

"That was months ago!"

She had no answer for that. How could she when she, herself, felt no defense?

"I was wrong."

"Damn straight," he muttered.

She moved her hand slightly, hoping to lower the window just an inch or two so the cold air could freeze out her increasingly persistent nausea. But even that slight movement sent pain careening through her, and she bit back a moan.

The landscape flashed by even faster. She didn't dare glance at the speedometer.

She rested her head against the leather seat. "I need to get hold of my parents." Whispering didn't seem so painful. "Tell them I'm going to be late."

"You're gonna be a helluva lot more than late. And that should be the least of your worries right now. What the hell were you thinking? You shouldn't even be riding in your condition."

"I've ridden all of my life. My obstetrician said there was no reason I couldn't continue to do so as long as I was careful."

"And that's a perfect description for what you did today with that infernal horse."

"That infernal horse is helping to pay my bills!"

"If you'd have told me you were pregnant, you wouldn't have to be worrying about your bills." His voice was tight. Full of anger. "Christ, J.D. Did you think I wouldn't take care of you?"

She'd known that he would. That his sense of responsibility would have ensured financial support for his child. And that would be as far as it would go.

Responsibility. But not love.

"I can take care of myself and this baby without you throwing money our way."

"Yeah." His voice was flat. "You've proved that so well today."

She angled her head carefully to look out the window away from him. He was right, so what could she say?

Neither one of them spoke for the rest of the drive that he made in about a third of the time it should have taken. It was a wonder that he didn't get stopped for speeding, but she supposed that her cousin-in-law Max, who was the sheriff, had a light roster of deputies on duty because of the holiday.

It wasn't as if she had to give Jake directions to the hospital, either, since it was right on the highway heading straight into town. Ignoring the signs that warned *ambulances only,* he pulled beneath the overhang that protected the emergency room entrance and came around to open her door.

She started to protest that she could walk on her own when he lifted her out of her seat, but the words died when he gave her a tight look.

His expression was almost the same as Zach's had been when Jake had said everything would be all right.

The first face she saw when he carried her through the entrance was her cousin, Courtney, who was a nurse at the hospital. Her eyes widened at the sight of them, and she hurried forward with a wheelchair. "What happened?"

"She was thrown. Something's wrong with her shoulder and she's pregnant." His gaze moved to J.D. again. "I suppose they all know that, though," he concluded. "Everyone gets to hear the truth except me."

"Jake—"

Courtney's lovely face was troubled as she took in the exchange. "Bring her on back," she said when it was clear that Jake had no intention of setting J.D. in the wheelchair. She hit a switch low on the wall and the double doors leading from the waiting room swung wide. "The first bed on your right. I'll be right there."

All of the beds in the emergency room were empty except for one on the far side that had a curtain drawn around it. Jake lowered J.D. onto the first bed they came to. She barely had a moment to exhale her relief—because being carried wasn't exactly the most comfortable of positions right then—when Courtney appeared again.

"I thought you were off today," J.D. told her.

"I was. One of the other nurses has the flu, so I got called in. Fortunately, I like the leftovers from Thanksgiving just as well." With a practiced tug, she swung the privacy curtain around the bed area and set a blank chart on the small counter next to the sink. "Did you lose consciousness when you fell?" She turned to J.D. and began to gently work the coat sleeve off her uninjured side.

"No."

"No."

Jake answered at the same time J.D. did and her gaze tangled with his.

Courtney managed to get off that sleeve, but J.D. was wringing wet with sweat by the time she finished. "I'm going to cut through the other sleeve," Courtney said. "It'll be easier on you."

J.D. was too breathless to argue. The coat had been damaged plenty well by Bonneville already. Her cousin peppered her with a stream of questions as she attacked the sleeve with a pair of deadly looking scissors. "Any cramping? You haven't been able to check for spotting, I imagine. Describe the pain in your shoulder. Sharp? Dull? Hot?"

J.D. answered, holding her arm tightly across her chest. If she didn't breathe too deeply or move too much, she thought she might escape passing out. "No cramps." Surely, she'd be able to tell even above the racking pain that was radiating from her shoulder in widening waves.

Her cousin didn't even attempt to unbutton the flannel shirt J.D. wore beneath the coat. She simply sliced through it and spread the fabric away from her shoulder. The fact that her action left J.D.'s unfettered breasts perfectly bare was only an inconvenient embarrassment where she was concerned.

There was such fiery pain exploding from J.D.'s shoulder that she figured her hot face could be taken as part of the package. But Jake wasn't giving her bare breasts even the faintest glance. His eyes were on her shoulder. "God," he muttered, looking oddly pale.

"At a guess, I'm going to say you dislocated it." Courtney snatched a packet out of the cupboard below the sink and squeezed it a few times before settling it gently against the offended joint.

J.D. gritted her teeth. The light weight of the pack was excruciatingly cold. "I may have to make you pay for this someday, Court."

Her cousin didn't turn a single hair on her unfairly beautiful blond head. "I know it hurts." She finally draped a cotton hospital gown over J.D.'s torso and with the finesse that nurses must learn in school, whisked off J.D.'s boots and the rest of her clothing without dislodging the cotton a single inch.

J.D. focused on the bump of her feet beneath the thin blanket that Courtney spread across her from the waist down after she'd stuck her clothing in a bin beneath the bed. "Dr. Keegan's your OB, right?" She barely waited for J.D.'s nod. "I'll get a call in to her right away. But Dr. Jackman will be with you as soon as he can. He's in the middle of stitching up a hand." Courtney shook her head a little. "Turkey-carving accident."

Turkey.

"I need to call my parents."

"I'll take care of it," Courtney assured and stepped outside of the curtain. "Yell if you need anything."

"There's only *one* doctor here?" Jake paced the close confines within the curtained area as soon as her cousin was gone. "What the hell kind of third-world hospital is this?"

"One that amply meets the needs of Weaver and its surrounding communities," J.D. returned wearily. "Just because it's not up to your standards doesn't mean it's a bad hospital. My aunt Rebecca runs the place, if you must know."

"Did you ever plan to tell me?"

She opened her mouth, but uncertainty strangled her vocal cords. "I don't know," she finally admitted.

His jaw canted to one side then slowly centered, though a muscle continued to tick alongside it. "At least that's *one* thing I believe you mean."

"I'm sorry."

But at that, Jake didn't look at all convinced. The curtain rings rattled again, and he looked over his shoulder as the white-coated doctor entered and introduced himself. Dr. Jackman took one quick look at J.D.'s shoulder and scribbled on the chart that Courtney had left behind. "We'll get you into X-ray as soon as we check the baby," he said, then glanced at Jake. "Would you rather your husband wait outside while I examine you?"

"He's not my husband," J.D. said.

"Sorry." The gray-haired doctor took it in stride. "Never know these days when it comes to couples." He rolled the low metal stool to the foot of the bed and sat down on it. "We need to do a pelvic, though, so—"

Jake silently left the curtained area.

J.D. wished that she could have called him back. Wished that they *were* a couple.

But now that was something that had never been further from reality. And she had no one to blame but herself for that.

Fortunately, the pelvic exam, followed by an ultrasound that Dr. Keegan arrived in time to supervise, assured J.D. that her pregnancy was mercifully unharmed by her fall.

"Does this mean I shouldn't have that ultrasound I already scheduled for next week?"

The doctor smiled faintly as she scribbled on J.D.'s chart. "No, though I don't think it will be necessary. I want to see you in my office, anyway, though. Just to follow up on that little fellow."

Tears collected in the corners of her eyes. "It *is* a boy."

"You told me before the test did," Dr. Keegan reminded. "Congratulations, Mom. Now, I'm getting back to my Thanksgiving dinner, and you are getting that shoulder taken care of." She surrendered J.D. to another technician who wheeled J.D. to the radiology department.

That X-ray confirmed the more obvious diagnosis that her shoulder was, indeed, dislocated. Once it was *relocated,* the worst of the pain eased off.

It just made it that much easier to feel the pain centered somewhere around her heart.

By then, the emergency room was practically filled with members of J.D.'s family who all knew now, without a question, that Jake was the father of the baby she carried.

Despite her insistence that she was fine and didn't want to interrupt the big family Thanksgiving dinner, they'd shown up anyway.

"We had to see with our own eyes that you're okay," Maggie said again in needless explanation. She and Angeline hovered next to J.D.'s bed while Courtney helped her dress again in her jeans and a borrowed surgical scrub top, followed up with a sling that she was going to have to wear for the next several weeks.

"Some Thanksgiving it's turned out to be." J.D. let out a relieved breath when Courtney was finished with her adjusting.

"You fell off a horse and your baby is still fine," Angeline reminded. With J.D. decent again, she pulled open the curtain around the bed. "Frankly, I think it's a wonderful Thanksgiving."

It was a good reminder that J.D. truly did have something to be thankful for, even if she'd irrevocably ruined any chance with Jake. But she still couldn't help looking for him the second that curtain was removed.

Her brother was there. Angeline's husband, Brody. A handful of aunts and uncles and other cousins. But there was no sign of Jake.

Daniel immediately moved forward to help her off the high bed, and the lot of them began the slow procession out of the emergency room. She stopped at the desk, expecting to sign paperwork of some sort since visits to the E.R. were generally accompanied by a bill. "Don't I need to sign something?"

Courtney was doing double duty at the desk, too. "Nope. Jake took care of everything before he left."

J.D. turned away. It would have been a more promising sign if he'd have ignored those details and chosen to stay with her.

But that was like wishing for the moon.

"Why don't you come and stay with your father and me," Maggie suggested when they reached her parents' SUV. All around them, vehicles bearing the rest of the clan were departing, heading back to the Double-C to continue on with the day's festivities.

"I'd rather be at home. I have things I have to take care of there."

"Someone else can take over for a while," Daniel said. "Your brother. Ryan." He was silent for a minute. "Jake; if he knows what's good for him."

She leaned her head back against the seat and closed her eyes. For the first time in her life, she didn't have horses at the forefront of her priorities. "The horses are my responsibility. Not Jake's."

She heard her father snort, and Maggie softly murmured, "Not now, Daniel."

"Why not now," he countered. "The guy's the father of my grandchild, for God's sake."

"I know that."

"Well, I *didn't,* until today," he muttered. "Any other little jewels of information you're keeping quiet about, Maggie Mae?"

"It was J.D.'s place to tell everyone when she was ready," Maggie returned without heat. "And you'd agree with me if you weren't irritated that you didn't figure it out for yourself first."

"I'm sure Ryan will help," J.D. told them, desperate to end the subject.

"If you won't stay with us, then I'll stay with you at your place," Maggie said.

J.D. loved her mother dearly, but the only thing she wanted was to be left alone. To let her heart bleed out in private. She would have argued if she could have summoned the energy.

Instead, she sat there, pretending to doze off because it was simply the easiest path.

When they arrived at her place, there was no sign of Jake's truck. It was proof that she'd held out some small hope that he would be there when her stomach sank to new depths. There also was no sign of Susan and the boys.

Her dad helped her inside while Maggie hurried ahead to her bedroom upstairs. There, she helped J.D. off with her boots and jeans again. "Do you want a nightgown?"

The idea of removing the sling and the scrub top was more than J.D. could stand. She shook her head and climbed awkwardly into the bed her mother had pulled back. She worked the quilt up to her nose with her good hand. "I don't want you and Dad being mad at each other over me."

Maggie sat carefully on the side of the bed. "We're not mad at each other. Your father's just feeling protective. It's what fathers do." She was silent for a moment. "Are you in love with him?"

She meant Jake, of course.

J.D.'s nose burned. Her vision glazed. "It doesn't matter. He doesn't love me." The sling with her bent arm was folded across her abdomen.

"Is that why you didn't tell him about the baby?"

"No!" Or was it? She was so confused about everything that she wasn't even sure about that any longer. "He won't let himself love this baby." He would never allow himself to feel that sense of protection that her father did.

"Are you so certain of that?" Maggie smoothed the edge of the quilt beneath J.D.'s chin. "Before he left the hospital, he looked beside himself."

"He's angry that I didn't tell him."

"A reasonable reaction," Maggie murmured mildly. "That doesn't mean he won't love the baby."

"You haven't seen him with his sons." J.D. pressed her good arm over her eyes. "They're dying for his love, Mom. But he won't give it."

"Then why'd he bring them here for Thanksgiving?"

Her mother wasn't asking anything that she hadn't already asked herself. Which only confirmed that her silence about their child was even more unforgivable. "I thought I had him all figured out, but…" She trailed off, miserably. "Now, I don't know anything." She dropped her arm. "Why couldn't I be more like you and less like my father?"

"I think you're very much like Daniel, actually," Maggie said, seeming a little amused. "You're both as stubborn as the day is long."

"I meant Joe Green."

Her mother blinked, seeming startled. "How on earth do you think you're like Joe?"

"He screwed up with the people he was supposed to love, too. He lied. He cheated."

"Oh, J.D." Maggie smoothed her hand over J.D.'s head as if she were still a little girl. "The only thing I believe you inherited from Joe were his green eyes."

"But *you'd* have never made such a mess of things the way I have."

"There are plenty of messes I can take credit for. That's what being human is about. The question is how you go about cleaning them up. You're a smart woman. I'm sure you'll find a solution."

J.D. shifted slightly and winced at the pain. "How's there a solution to loving a man who doesn't want to be loved?"

"Well." Maggie's gaze softened. "I found that loving him anyway was pretty effective." She pushed off the bed. "You need your pain medication."

She left, leaving J.D. completely bemused. A short while later, heavier footsteps came back up and she braced herself for a round with her well-intentioned father.

But it was Jake who came striding into the room.

She stared at him for an interminable moment. He'd changed clothes. His soiled silk shirt replaced by another. His trousers by black jeans. "What are you doing here?"

He held up a glass of water and a prescription bottle. "Your parents left once I assured them both that I would be at your side. Your mother took me at my word. Your father looked like he would've preferred to kill me." He set the water glass on her nightstand and shook out a small round pill into his palm.

Yet he obviously wasn't cowed by either one of her parents, or he wouldn't be there.

"What about the boys?"

"They're at the motel with Susan." He held out his palm. "Take it."

She chewed the inside of her lip, watching him warily. "You don't have to stay here with me."

"When I say I'll do something, I do it." He held out the water glass, too.

He did it, whether he wanted to or not. "I don't want pain pills."

"I called Dr. Keegan. She said it wouldn't hurt the baby." His palm didn't budge from where it hovered three inches in front of her nose. "Riding around the way you do is a helluva lot more dangerous, as today ought to show."

She grimaced and plucked the pill off his palm, tossing it back with a mouthful of water before handing him back the glass.

"Drink the rest."

Feeling not much older than Zach and Connor, she took back the glass and forced down the water. "Satisfied?"

"Not even remotely." He set the glass on the nightstand and took a seat in the upholstered wing chair opposite her bed, where she couldn't fail to see him.

"Staying by her side" took on a whole new nightmarish quality.

She closed her eyes but the image of him sitting there, his hands casually folded together across his fine leather belt, seemed imprinted on her brain.

"The baby will have the same kind of trust fund that the boys have." His words dropped like stones.

She opened her eyes. "It's a boy," she whispered.

His jaw whitened a little but he continued, as if she hadn't spoken. "I'll contact my lawyer to set it up. The papers can be here by courier in a few days. Essentially it will provide for all of his educational and medical needs until he's 25. The principal will be distributed to him then. He'll also receive an equal number of shares in Forco."

Her throat tightened with protests that she knew would be futile. Every word he said seemed to pound a nail in the coffin of hope that her foolish heart had been defiantly nourishing.

"You'll receive a monthly allowance—"

She stiffened. "No. Absolutely not."

"—that should more than provide for your living expenses and the like. In the event of your marriage, the amount is adjusted slightly, but will never be rescinded."

She looked away, not even able to blame the sharp pang

inside her on her shoulder. "Set up whatever you want for the baby," she said dully. "But I don't need or want your money."

"You're still going to get it."

"Is this how you treated your ex-wife?"

"I never trusted my ex-wife," he said after a moment. "I trusted you."

The impact of that hurt far worse than when she'd hit the cold, hard ground. "I thought I was doing the right thing for everyone."

"Keeping me away from your child is one thing." He propped his boot on the opposite knee. "That's the good sense of a mother talking. Not telling me he exists is something else."

"Until now, you'd made it clear that being a father wasn't anything that you *wanted* to be."

"Being a father isn't anything that I *should* be," he corrected expressionlessly. "But you're carrying my…son. So, you'd better know it all."

The pain pill was taking quick effect, making her hands and feet feel oddly disconnected. "Know what all?"

"My father, rest his cursed soul, was a mean son of a bitch. When he was sober, he made sure you knew how much he regretted your birth with words. And when he wasn't sober, he made sure you knew with his fists."

Horror sucked through her, even penetrating the pain pill's haze. "Your father beat you?"

"Until I was big enough to hit him back."

She thought of all the rumors and gossip that had been rife at Forrest's Crossing. Not once had such a thing even been hinted at. "Did your mother know?"

"Yes."

She felt sick. "And she still left you and your sisters there with him?"

"Obviously. I was almost ten when she booked."

About the same age that Zach and Connor were now and she ached all over again for the boy he'd been. And the man he'd become. "What about Susan? Did she know? Why didn't anyone stop it? Step in?"

His lips twisted. "Because nobody crossed Jacob Forrest, Sr. And, yeah, Susan knew. She couldn't divert him every time, but she made attempts." His gaze slanted to her. "Just one big happy family we were. I made the mistake once of thinking I could have some sort of normal life when I married Tiff. I was wrong." He lowered his boot and rose from the chair. "I can judge a business deal. I can sometimes judge horseflesh. But when it comes to relationships?" His lips tightened as he reached for the door. "I still can't judge a damned thing."

Then he turned on his heel. And left.

She wanted to call him back.

But what good were words now?

Chapter Fourteen

Jake was sitting at J.D.'s kitchen table with his laptop, forcing himself through the correspondence his secretary had sent him, when his aunt arrived the next morning with the boys in tow.

Zach and Connor barely offered a grudging hello before they escaped back outside, leaving Susan to dump an enormous camera bag on the table. "How's J.D.?"

"Still sleeping." At least she had been when he'd checked on her a short while earlier. Just as she'd been sleeping the dozen other times he'd checked on her.

When he'd realized he was falling asleep in that unexpectedly feminine wing chair across from her bed while he'd watched J.D. sleep, he'd made himself go down to the living-room couch.

It was too short, but not quite the torture device that the too-small chair was.

"What do you intend to do about her?"

"Take care of the baby the same way I have the boys."

"I didn't ask about the baby," she pointed out mildly.

"There's nothing else to talk about *but* the baby," he said flatly.

"Don't pretend with me, Jake. I know what you're doing here."

"Keeping an eye on Latitude."

She laughed outright. "Darling, there's never been a horse that matters so much to you that you'd rearrange your entire life like you have for these past three weeks. You're here because of J.D. There's no harm in admitting that you care for her."

He tapped out a terse response to one of his e-mails, hit Send and closed the computer. "There's nothing to admit."

She gave him a pitying look. "And the baby? I suppose you plan to put up the money to pay for the best of everything. But not put out your own feelings."

"The Forrest way." He lifted the coffee mug in a macabre toast. Where had feelings ever gotten him? The only times he'd trusted in them, they'd bitten him on the ass.

His aunt pointed her finger at him. "Don't use the excuse that it's in your blood. You're thirty-seven years old. You have every advantage in life to make the choices you want. Jacob wasn't the best father. We all admit that. But he's been gone for the better part of twenty years!"

"And the memory lives on," he shot back. "You're as guilty of it as the rest of us. You haven't moved on, either. The old man should've just married you. You were his hostess at the parties he liked to throw. You managed his household. Instead of photographing babies, you should have had kids of your own. Instead, you got stuck raising us after our mother washed her hands of us."

"And if I'd have done a better job, maybe you wouldn't be terrified of being a parent!"

"I'm not terrified." His voice was flat. "I'm realistic. And I want you to take the boys back to California today. This was only supposed to be for the holiday. They're not going to care that I cut it short."

His aunt slowly pulled out a chair and sat down. "I think you're wrong. And frankly, I'd hoped the holiday was just an excuse. That it would lead to more. You've been here for three weeks. I'd thought maybe you were going to change things for good."

He got up from his chair and refilled his mug with coffee he didn't want. "I let J.D. make me think they needed to be here. With me." And all the while, she'd been hiding her pregnancy.

Through the window over the sink, he could see Zach and Connor standing on the bottom rail of the corral next to the barn. The only horse out there was Ziggy. He and Ryan had managed to get Bonneville stabled the night before. But Jake hadn't wanted to give the horse another opportunity to fight Ziggy by turning him out again that morning.

"Just because she didn't tell you about the baby doesn't mean she's not right about the boys. They do need their family, Jake, not just a boarding school they hate, and the attention of their mother's housekeeper. Start being a father to those boys. And to that baby that young woman upstairs is carrying. You have a whole new opportunity to be everything that you've convinced yourself you can't be. It's not too late."

From upstairs, they both heard a soft sound.

J.D. was stirring.

"Just take the boys back to California, Susan."

"No." She rose from her chair and began buttoning up her coat again.

"What do you mean, *no*?"

"It's a simple word," she said evenly. "They're *your* sons. If you want them in California, you'll have to take them there, because I refuse to."

He narrowed his eyes. "You've never refused me anything."

"And clearly, that was a mistake. I didn't stay at Forrest's

Crossing after Olivia left Jacob because of him. I stayed because of you and your sisters. Because I loved all three of you. I didn't have to have children of my own because *you* were the children of my heart. I wasn't stuck. I made my choices. And I haven't always agreed with you, but I've never been disappointed in you. Not until now."

His jaw tightened. "This isn't the most convenient time for you to develop a stubborn streak, Susan."

She looked pained. "Better late than never. Don't worry, Jake. I'm not abandoning you with the boys. I'm simply refusing to take them back to California right now." She pulled a camera out of her bag and stomped out of the house.

He scraped his hands down his face.

Through the window over the sink, he saw her heading toward Zach and Con. Already, her camera was held up to her face.

He turned from the sight and went upstairs.

J.D., looking sleep-rumpled and leggy in just the drab green scrub top that barely reached her thighs, was coming out of the bathroom.

Her hair was a barely tamed mass of waves and she had a tiny smudge of toothpaste below the corner of her lips. But her eyes were alert and clear and they widened at the sight of him before she quickly turned toward her bedroom. "You're still here."

He followed her into the room. "I said I'd stay."

She bent over a low drawer, giving him a view of skimpy lace panties and shapely rear that he knew was completely un-intentional on her part.

Since he didn't pretend to be a gentleman, he didn't bother making himself look away before she straightened with a pair of jeans in her hand.

She shoved the drawer closed with her foot and looked at him through the reflection of the mirror above the dresser. "Well, I'm much better this morning, so there's no need for you to worry about that anymore."

"Your arm's still in a sling and will be for weeks."

"Thanks to those little pills, I can't even feel it right now. I'll manage."

He lifted an eyebrow. "Like you're going to manage to get those jeans on with one hand?"

Annoyance glinted in her eyes but he knew she realized the challenge facing her with just this one, ordinarily simple task.

She nevertheless sat on the foot of the tumbled bed and shook out the jeans, awkwardly bending forward as far as her contained arm would allow, attempting it, anyway.

He let her struggle until he heard her catch her breath in the obvious pain that she supposedly wasn't feeling, then he tugged the jeans out of her hands and crouched at her feet. "Lift."

"This is humiliating," she muttered.

He didn't budge. "You'll live." His voice was hard.

She huffed out a breath and lifted her feet so he could thread the jeans up her legs. When he reached her thighs, she stood, and he pulled the soft, well-worn denim up over her narrow hips and those all-but transparent panties.

Looking anywhere but at him, she gathered the hem of the scrub top higher around her hips so he could pull up the zipper.

The zip went up, but the button at the top was a no-go.

Suddenly face-to-face with the evidence of her pregnancy, his hands slowed.

His chest felt tight and he couldn't seem to stop himself from inexorably lowering the zip right back down again.

His thumb grazed over her abdomen and he felt the shimmer in her smooth flesh. "I should have noticed." Realized. Her deception aside, it now seemed obvious.

Her slender throat worked. "I made sure you wouldn't." She sucked in her lower lip just long enough to leave it wet and distracting. "I'm sorry."

"Are you?" His voice seemed to come from somewhere

deep inside him. "You're going to profit plenty from bearing a Forrest."

He felt her tense. "I shouldn't have kept it from you," she said unsteadily. "I know that. But not once have I earned a comment like *that*."

"Right. You're never about the money. Only about family. And feelings. And doing what's right. Saint J.D."

Tears glistened in her eyes and he hated himself just a little more.

He turned his hand until his palm rested on the small bulge of the child she carried.

"I grew up knowing that I was a carbon copy of my father. He said so. My mother—before she skipped—said so. I stepped into his shoes at Forco before I was even legal to drink. Everyone there said I was a chip off the block when I didn't drive the place into the ground, but actually made it even more successful."

"You can be a more successful father, too." Her voice was barely a whisper.

His gaze slowly dragged up from his darker palm pressed against her pale flesh. Despite everything, her nipples were hard points, easily discernable through the thin cotton top.

He hadn't touched her in weeks. But he hadn't stopped wanting to touch her, ever.

It didn't matter that his aunt was just outside with the boys. It didn't matter that J.D. had lied to him, or even that her arm was in a sling.

He wanted to slide her jeans back down her hips and take her, right then and there.

Maybe then he could get rid of this damn ache inside of him.

She exhaled softly and his gaze rose to her face.

She couldn't hide her expressions any more than he could hide the fact that he was rock hard. Pink rode her high cheekbones. Her eyes were even greener than they usually were.

Her narrow nostrils flared slightly and that minute smear of toothpaste beckoned, tauntingly.

His fingertips grazed the tempting edge of her lace panties. A centimeter more and he could reach beneath them.

Moments stretched to minutes. Minutes to forever.

Her flesh seemed to warm beneath his palm and he couldn't tell if the fire was burning in him, or her.

Or both.

He watched the pulse beating wildly at the base of her throat. "Do you want me to close the door?" he asked, his voice a little deeper. His tone a little harder.

Her head fell back slightly. Her damp eyes glowed between her thick eyelashes. The waving ends of her long hair tickled his arm. "What do you want to do? Prove how weak I am where you're concerned? Yes, I want you to close the door. But it won't solve anything."

It would solve plenty for him.

He went to the door and closed it. Flipped the tiny lock beneath the old-fashioned, porcelain knob.

Then he turned to face her. She hadn't moved a muscle. "I won't hurt you." Not her shoulder. Not the baby.

"I know."

But he could see in her eyes the same lie that was in him. Because he *could* hurt her. In so many ways. Since the night they'd made love at Forrest's Crossing, that fact had never been more apparent.

"And I won't love you," he added roughly.

Her eyes darkened. "I never believed you would," she whispered. But she slowly stepped toward him, stopping only when her bare toes were inches from the toes of his boots. Her lips lifted toward his. Her free hand settled, feather light, on his chest. "But you want me," she whispered. "So, touch me."

It was more challenge than invitation and he was suddenly wondering who was pushing whom.

He dropped his mouth to hers and flicked his tongue over that toothpaste dab.

She inhaled sharply and he angled his mouth over hers, taking everything that she offered.

Trying not to jostle her sore arm, he slid his arm around her hips and lifted her to the dresser. The collection of old-fashioned perfume bottles sitting on top of it jangled softly. The mirror above it swayed back a centimeter, the wood frame brushing the wall.

He smoothly pulled her jeans back down her legs and this time she didn't look at him as if it were the least bit humiliating.

"Help me with my sling."

They could leave it in place. It would probably be better if they did. He carefully worked it off, watching her face closely for signs of pain.

All he saw, though, was her desire.

It was like a drug to him. One that he knew enough to avoid. One that he couldn't.

He tossed the sling to the side and ran his hands beneath the top. Closed around her satiny waist. Her breath tumbled more unevenly over her parted lips when he dragged the cotton upward. Found the taut slopes of her breasts, the nipples that prodded the pads of his thumbs, seeming greedy for attention.

He exhaled roughly and started to lift the shirt higher, but she gave a soft huff and he immediately stopped.

"Sorry." She was the one who apologized.

He let the fabric slip out of his hands.

"No." She tilted her head, finding his lips with hers. Her left hand dragged at the buttons on his shirt. "I want it off. Everything. I want to feel you against me." She slipped her hand beneath his shirt, pushing at it.

He yanked off his shirt, scattering the last of the buttons

and tossed it aside. Taking his cue from the day before at the hospital, he closed his hands over the V-neck of her thin shirt and with a swift tug, rent the thin fabric right down the middle.

She let out a long, shaking breath. And still she didn't protest. Didn't back away. Just stared at him with those emerald eyes that haunted his sleep.

He could see her pulse beating in her throat as she slowly slid off the ruined shirt. It slid easily down her slender back.

Her shoulder was swollen. Angrily bruised.

He swore softly. "J.D."

"Don't even look there," she whispered, and lifted his clenched hand. She spread his fingers and pressed his palm to her racing heart. "Look here."

The ache inside him deepened. "Don't."

"Why not? You tell me the worst about your father, not because you want to share yourself with me. But because you want to prove that you're right. That you can't chance being any sort of father. Can't chance loving someone again. Can't expect someone to love *you* unless it's all wrapped up in dollars and cents."

"Stop."

"Or what?" Her head tilted back. Her hair streamed down her shoulders. "*You'll* stop?" She boldly grazed her knuckles down his straining fly. "I don't think so. We have it all on the table, right? You won't love me. So, just take what you want from me, Jake. I give it."

He grabbed her hand, pressing it firmly against him. Seeing the flare in her eyes. "Because you *want* me."

"Because I *love* you."

He let go of her hand. "Don't try putting a prettier slant on it."

"Don't worry," she returned huskily. "Loving you isn't all that pretty right now."

They stared at each other for a long, tight moment.

"I don't know what the hell to do with you," he finally muttered.

She pulled his hands to her breasts. "Yes, you do."

He'd wanted to prove something but the only thing he was proving was that he was the weak one when it came to her. And she was right. He wasn't going to stop.

Couldn't make himself.

He cupped the weight of her breasts, newly aware of the differences her pregnancy had wrought. They were fuller. The crests darker. Even more seductive than what lived in his memories.

He lowered his mouth to them and she moaned softly, her head falling back to the mirror, her good hand sinking through his hair, holding him to her.

He tasted. He suckled. And she trembled harder, the little perfume bottles jangling again, when he kissed his way down her abdomen, no longer flat, but softly rounded, lushly erotic. Then he reached that narrow hank of lace and drew that, too, away from the sweet flesh that was damp and warm, just for him.

She gasped, her racehorse legs parting as he tasted her there. Boldly. His hunger only growing as she shuddered and abruptly convulsed beneath him, her fingers clenching his hair.

The mirror rattled softly. A little glass bottle tipped over, falling undamaged to the braided rug beneath them. Jake shoved off the rest of his clothes and closed his hands around her hips, urging her toward him though she hardly needed urging. Her thighs clasped his and he took her weight, sliding deeply.

Her eyes flew open, staring into his and he felt oddly disembodied, swallowed whole by those emerald depths.

But then her legs wrapped around him and she seemed to tighten even more as she tilted her hips against him, and he came back to earth with a soaring crash.

And then there was nothing but the blind need to go deeper. Slower. Harder. Faster.

Another bottle tipped off the dresser. Her mouth, open, hot, pressed against his shoulder, stifling the sobbing breaths she couldn't hold back. Her good arm gathered him closer, as if she knew every cell in his body was gathering together; as if hers were, as well.

Then she cried out, softly, muffled, long and low as she shuddered. And the intimate quakes gloved him, pulling him with earth-shattering force headlong after her. His teeth ground together as he forced himself not to crush her while an endless pleasure ripped through him, draining himself inside her.

After, when his legs stopped feeling like wet cotton and his heart didn't feel like it was going to explode, he carried her to the bed and settled her carefully in the center, drawing the sheet over her beautiful body.

Her eyes were wet.

"The stalls need mucking out," he said. "And I've got a conference call in a few hours."

She paled, but didn't look away from him. "Okay."

He pulled on his shirt. Made a face when he got to the missing buttons and shoved the shirt tails into his jeans. Then he yanked open her closet door and pulled out the first flannel shirt he came to. He dropped it on the mattress next to her, and proving not only to himself but to her what a bastard he truly was, he walked out of the room.

He'd solved absolutely nothing.

Chapter Fifteen

It took a while, but J.D. finally gathered some composure together after Jake's exit and went downstairs.

She'd managed to dress herself, but there was no way she was able to pull on the sling without assistance.

She had no intention of asking him. There wasn't a breath of privacy between them anymore, but her pride still crept around her, even if it did feel more like a hole-ridden sweater than armor.

"You're looking much better this morning," his aunt greeted when she reached the living room.

"My shoulder feels better." It was all she could do not to blush when her body still ached from Jake's possession and her heart still ached from his rejection. "It's tender but nothing like yesterday." She lifted the sling slightly. "Would you mind terribly?"

Susan immediately set down her camera and came over to her. Between the two of them, they managed to get J.D.'s pained arm secured again. Then J.D. went to the kitchen and pulled down a glass, setting it on the counter. She opened the refrigerator door, popping off the lid of the milk jug before pulling it out to pour herself a glass. "Have you seen Jake?" she asked casually when Susan followed her.

"He blew through here a little while ago." Susan was holding her fancy camera again, pressing buttons, scrolling through the digital images. She held one up for J.D. to see. "Look at this one."

J.D. obediently looked. It was a close up of Zach sitting astride the fence as if he were bronc busting. "He's smiling."

"He's having fun. Both boys are."

J.D. just wanted to sit down and bawl. Instead, she forced down several gulps of milk. "Speaking of boys. Are they outside?"

"Yes. I checked on them a few minutes ago. They were still sitting on the fence. I made them promise on threat of creamed spinach that they wouldn't go inside the ring. I think they might actually listen, given what they saw could happen yesterday."

J.D. managed a small smile and choked down a little more milk. "Have you all had breakfast?"

"We ate at a little diner by the motel. They had wonderful cinnamon rolls."

"That would be Ruby's." J.D. pulled a granola bar out of the cupboard and slid off the wrapper. She wasn't hungry by any stretch, but knew she had to put some calories in. "Seriously good rolls," she agreed. "I, um, I want to go check on Latitude."

"Of course." Susan waved her hand slightly. "I don't need entertaining, dear. Go. Do what you need to do."

J.D. grimaced. If only she could figure out what that was. She pulled a heavyweight flannel jacket over her good arm as best as she could, and went outside.

The barn door was already wide open.

Jake's doing. She gathered her tattered pride closer around her. She had work to do in the barn even if he *was* already in there.

The boys were where Susan had said they'd be, on top of the fence. Threat of creamed spinach or not, J.D. figured it was only a matter of time before they were inside the ring.

"Zach. Con," she called. "Come into the barn."

The boys looked at her for a moment, deciding the merit of that. But their legs swung back over the fence and they hopped down, heading her way. They wore different colored down coats, but aside from that, they were as alike as two peas.

Connor didn't hide his curiosity as he followed her inside. The second Zach entered, he wrinkled his nose. "It stinks in here."

"It does smell like horse," J.D. agreed, surprised that she could feel even the slightest bit of amusement.

"What's that thing?" Connor was pointing at the horse sling. The complicated contraption of straps and webbing was rigged up with pulleys to one of the solid barn beams and it hung, ghostly empty, over the last stall.

"A horse sling. We fit it beneath and around Latitude to take the weight off his legs a few hours every day so he can heal up."

"Wonder if Mom's in something like that."

"Duh. Mom's in traction."

J.D. pointed to the wheelbarrow sitting by the tack room. "Roll that over to the first stall," she told the boys, clinging desperately to the comfort of practical matters. "And bring a pitchfork. It's hanging on a hook over there."

"What for?" Zach's gaze slid around to see what his father was doing.

"Gotta muck out all of the stalls I'm using. Have to keep the bedding clean for the horses. Which means we pick out the messed up straw and put down fresh," she translated. "Standing around in soiled stalls isn't healthy. Or good-smelling."

Zach grimaced. "Like cleaning out a big cat box?"

She stretched her lips. "Kind of."

With more enthusiasm than finesse, Connor was pushing the wheelbarrow toward her. "Zach and I are supposed t' clean Freckles' cat box during the summer but Lupe always did it for us, instead." His expression fell a little.

J.D. quickly caught one handle of the wheelbarrow before he could run over her foot, and redirected him a little. "Have you talked to your mom?"

"She's supposed to be outta the hospital by Christmas," Zach answered.

"And moving into a convalescent center," Jake inserted, surprising them all a little, judging by the way the boys started as noticeably as J.D. "It's still going to be a while before she's ready to go home."

"That's still good news though, right?" J.D. stopped next to Ziggy's empty stall and handed Zach the pitchfork. "Your mom is getting better." She pointed at the straw. "Have at it. Manure goes in the wheelbarrow in case you haven't figured that out on your own."

He looked like he wanted to argue. But he took the long handle. "Kind of hard to do this with only one hand, I suppose."

"Yes." She wanted to brush her hands over his rumpled hair but controlled the urge, knowing he wouldn't be likely to appreciate it. Offering her heart on a platter to one Forrest man a day was as much as she could stand. "I'd be really grateful for the help."

His lips pressed together and wriggled around a little. Then he turned to face the task. "This is totally gross," he said under his breath. "Connor's gotta do the next one."

Judging by Connor's rapt attention, she figured his twin wasn't going to argue too much.

She left them and braced herself to move over to Latitude's stall. "They're good kids," she offered. "Did you ever have trouble telling them apart?"

"No." Jake was slowly running his hand down Latitude's back leg. "Zach always had fire in his eyes. Connor had dreams in his. Even when they were babies."

Her heart squeezed hard. Just then he didn't sound at all like the closed-off man he claimed to be.

"He's swelling."

Her thoughts screeched to a halt.

Frowning, she stepped into the stall, settling her hand on Latitude's rump and sliding it down his thigh as she crouched awkwardly beside Jake. "Where?"

"Above the cast."

She slowly felt her way down the colt's hock. It felt warmer than it should have. Her fingers crept a little farther. She could barely slip them beneath the edge of the cast.

The day before and for the last week at least, she'd been able to slide nearly her entire palm beneath the cast. She skipped over the cast to the base of it. Found more swelling there, too.

Latitude's head angled around, giving her a wounded look. He nickered warningly and lifted his foot, obviously trying to move away from her touch.

She stifled a worried curse. "We need to get Evan over here."

"I'll call him." Jake helped her stand. Before he left the stall, he buttoned the top of her jacket at her neck so it wouldn't fall off. His touch was grimly impersonal.

It still left her feeling shattered.

J.D. moved around to Latitude's head, brushing her hands over him. "What's going on, Lat," she whispered.

His eyes just looked back at her, as liquid and soulful as ever. The colt blew out a soft breath and she sighed, pressing her forehead to his.

The boys had progressed through half the stalls before Evan arrived and J.D. had already taken Latitude's temperature, confirming that it was elevated.

"Sorry it took so long," Evan said as he strode into the barn. "Was over at Jefferson's. He's got a mare who's colicky." He set his large kit on the ground inside Latitude's stall and turned to examine the colt. J.D. could tell just by the soberness of Evan's face that he wasn't pleased. "What's his temp?"

She told him while her stomach tightened even more. "He hasn't run a higher temp for nearly three weeks. He was fine until yesterday," she said. "He was in the ring with Bonneville. Trotting some."

"He stopped short when we kept him from getting out," Jake added.

J.D. trembled. "It's my fault. If I had kept my seat on Ziggy, we'd have noticed before now." Instead, everyone's attention had turned to her.

Jake looked impatient. "If you're gonna blame someone, blame me. I bedded him down last night."

Evan just "hmmed," leaving whatever his opinion was out of it. He probed around the cast and again Latitude tried shifting away. Evan lifted his hoof. Listened to his heart. Examined every single inch of the colt. Made notes on his chart, and then flipped open the case he'd brought. He tossed Jake a protective apron and took another out for himself. J.D. rolled over the stand that Evan had been leaving there for convenience's sake so he could attach the portable radiograph unit to it, then moved well away from the area while the two men took several painstaking X-rays.

J.D. hadn't thought the day could be any more of a rollercoaster than it already had been, but she was wrong when Evan shared what he'd found. Two of the screws that had been used to stabilize the bone were bent and working their way out.

"It probably happened yesterday when he was being so active," he said. "And the cast is going to have to come off to be certain, but I'm pretty sure he's developing an abscess. That would account for the new infection." Evan looked at them both. "We'll have to get him over to my clinic. I can do what I can, but you probably should call in Dr. Windsor. I've done a lot of surgeries, but he's a helluva lot more qualified for this than I am."

Jake looked grim. "Trailer him up," he told the vet. His gaze skipped over J.D.'s. "I'll get hold of Windsor."

J.D. watched him stride out of the barn. The screws could be replaced, she knew. And an abscess treated with antibiotics. She just prayed that they didn't find anything worse.

J.D.'s parents showed up while she and Evan were settling Latitude in his horse trailer. Without needing details, they grasped the gravity of the situation. They gathered Susan and the boys and insisted they come over to their house where they would all be more comfortable while Jake and J.D. dealt with matters here.

Since Jake had arrived in Weaver with Latitude, J.D. had usually been able to push the possibility of the colt not recovering to the back of her mind. He'd been doing so well. Everything had looked so promising. They'd been so careful to guard against contamination, hoping to prevent just this thing.

Now, as she sat next to Jake in his truck as they drove the trailer to Evan's veterinary clinic in Weaver, it seemed as if the days of promise had never been.

As empty as the road into Weaver had been the day before when Jake sped her to the hospital, now there seemed a stream of traffic and she realized absently that it was Thanksgiving Friday.

The busiest shopping day of the year, even in little old Weaver, Wyoming. It may have felt like her life was in some painful holding pattern, but the rest of the world was breezing right along.

They offloaded Latitude at the clinic and Evan moved him to a pristine stall. He started him on antibiotics, doing what he could for the colt until the surgeon arrived, which wasn't until the next morning.

They didn't get the surgery underway until afternoon. Fortunately, Evan's clinic was well-equipped and he assisted Dr.

Windsor while J.D. paced in the waiting room and Jake observed through a window.

It took hours, but was nowhere near as long as the wait had been for the colt's first surgery in New York. Jake came to find her when it was over. "They drained the abscess. Changed out about half the screws and put on another cast."

"And?" She could tell by his face that there was more.

His dark eyes were flat. "He's developing acute laminitis in his right foot. Evan saw no evidence of it yesterday. It's fast and it's bad."

Her knees gave way and she sank into a hard, plastic chair.

"Windsor gives him about a twenty-percent chance at this point," he added evenly.

She tightened her jaw, keeping her teeth from chattering. A fifty-percent chance was a coin toss. Anything less was almost certain not to end well.

Since the moment Jake had found out J.D. was pregnant, it seemed as if everything was spiraling out of control.

"Come on. I'll drive you home."

She shook her head. "I'm not leaving Latitude."

"He's not even out of his anesthesia, yet."

"I'm not abandoning him now, Jake. For God's sake, I was there when he was foaled!"

He grimaced, but let the matter lie.

She stayed at the clinic for the rest of the day, even after Latitude was safely out of his anesthesia and Dr. Windsor left. The surgeon would be staying in town overnight to evaluate Latitude the following morning, but J.D. would have had to have been blind not to see that he considered the situation hopeless. Evan went out for a while, but would be back shortly. Latitude wouldn't be left unattended for the next fore-seeable hours.

His condition was too critical.

Her dad came by, delivering containers of Thanksgiving-day leftovers for her and Jake that Maggie had sent. Her father sat down on the floor beside her where she was sitting next to Latitude's stall, her food untouched next to her.

"You've gotta eat, J.D.," he murmured quietly. "No matter what happens to Latitude—good or bad—you have a baby you've got to nourish."

She pressed her forehead against the wall beside her. There was no need for a gate on the stall.

Latitude wasn't going anywhere.

Right now, he was showing how smart he was by lying down in the deep sand that they'd spread in his stall to provide a more cushioned surface. Being off his feet for even a minimal amount of time was a good thing. His pain was being managed and his eyes followed every movement around him with some age-old acceptance that she couldn't bring herself to share. "I was just patting myself on the back the other day that we'd dodged this bullet. Thinking how nearly ideal his recovery has been."

"All you can do is the best you can do," Daniel said. "And I've never seen you do less than your best. Not with any horse."

"I keep thinking about Bonita."

Daniel sighed. "You hated me for putting her down."

"She couldn't be saved. I know that. Letting her go was the kindest thing. But I loved her."

He pressed his lips to her head. "I know."

She plucked at a loose thread on her sling. "Maybe it would have been better for everyone if Jake hadn't brought Latitude here." She let out a breath. "The collisions that keep occurring might not have happened at all."

"Some things are destined to collide no matter what. Looks to me like you and Jake are one of them. He followed you here, didn't he?"

"Only because of Latitude."

"Are you sure?"

"Positive. Why can't things be easy like it was with you and Mom?"

He laughed and Latitude's ears perked. "Honey, you have no idea. Love doesn't necessarily hit easily in this family. But for us smarter ones, we manage to work our way around to what matters regardless of how impossible it seems, and then to hang on to it with everything we've got." He pushed himself to his feet and ruffled the top of her hair. "Now eat."

There was no real reason for her to feel better once he left again. But she did. She slowly pulled the tray of food onto her lap and stuck her fork into a chunk of turkey.

She ate half of what was on the plate, then clumsily shifted to her knees, and made her way to her feet. She fancied she saw humor in Latitude's eyes as he watched her ungainly movements and then he heaved a tired breath and closed his eyes.

She found Jake in Evan's office. He was staring at the cell phone in his hand and judging by the amount of food left on his plate, his appetite was about on a par with hers.

"Miguel will be running Platinum at Santa Anita in January."

J.D. winced a little. But that was the name of the game. Jake wanted winning horses. Miguel was going to deliver. "I'm sure he'll do well." Platinum was Jake's best chance at fulfilling his Derby aspirations. "I guess you told him the latest about Lat."

"Yeah."

"He wanted you to cut your losses from the get-go."

"Yeah."

Something in his expression made her aching heart sink even further. "Have you already made up your mind, then? You're not even going to wait to see if the laminitis can be resolved?"

"I'll wait until Windsor's evaluation tomorrow."

She swallowed past the knot in her throat. "And no later. He shows improvement by then or else."

"I have to draw a line somewhere, J.D."

"But we're managing his pain! If it gets to the point where we can't, then—" She broke off, shaking her head. "Just because it's not how you saw him turning out doesn't mean he can't have a good life. A blanket of roses matters to *you*, Jake. Not to him!"

"He's a racehorse, J.D., that's not gonna race again. Face it."

"But racing isn't all there has to be for his life."

"You want him puttering around in the ring beside your barn, chasing butterflies with the likes of Bonneville?"

"There are worse things. Has he seemed unhappy to you since you brought him to Weaver?" She might as well have been asking if Jake had been unhappy in Weaver for the way she felt braced for his answer.

Jake's lips pressed together.

She tucked her tongue between her teeth for a long moment. Curled her fist. "Even after everything that's happened since you came to Weaver, you won't let yourself look beyond what *is* to see what *could be*. You'd still rather sit here, clinging to your cynicism and the importance of your almighty dollar, than open yourself up to even the slightest possibility of something different!"

"It's too late for that."

"You're wrong." She looked at him, wishing with every fiber of her being that he'd show some crack, some hint that she wasn't yearning for the impossible.

But the chances of that seemed even less than Latitude's chances were.

"It's never too late," she finally said before walking out the door, "when it comes to someone you love."

Chapter Sixteen

It wasn't easy, but around midnight, Jake got J.D. to finally leave the clinic. Probably only because he'd found her sound asleep in the stall with Latitude, her blond waves mingling with the strands of the colt's black mane.

She was silent as they drove back to her house.

Probably because she'd already talked herself out.

She was a smart woman. Maybe she finally recognized a lost cause even if she had been reckless enough to think she loved him.

Her admission haunted him.

She'd see soon enough that betting on him that way was as futile as betting on Latitude.

He went inside with her, flatly telling her that she was not going to check the horses when Ryan had already been and gone to take care of the chore for her.

She looked like she wanted to argue, but fatigue was framing her eyes and instead, she turned and trudged up the stairs.

He followed, and she stiffly allowed him to help her out of the sling and the button-down blouse she wore and replace it with a worn, oversize and faded T-shirt.

It was a galaxy away from sexy lingerie and it still left him aching.

Rather, *she* left him aching. Mostly in the area of his heart.

With the sling back in place, she turned away from him. "I'll manage the rest." Her voice was remote.

Given what had happened the last time he'd helped her with her jeans, that was a good thing.

Maybe he didn't trust his own willpower or maybe he couldn't take sleeping beneath her roof and not sleeping with *her*, but he let himself out into the dark again and drove back into town.

It was late, but it was a Saturday night on a holiday weekend and the lights were on at several places as he drove down Main toward the motel. Even there, the parking lot was full.

Feeling wearier than he could ever recall feeling, he quietly unlocked the door to his room and went inside. He wanted a shower and a bed and oblivion from the turmoil that was inside his head. But when the dim light from the parking lot shined in on the plain room, both of the beds there were neatly made. And clearly unoccupied.

He frowned. The connecting door to Susan's room was firmly closed. He went to push it open, figuring the boys must be in there instead, but the door didn't budge.

Fine. Whatever. They were in the other room. Locked him out. She wanted privacy. Or she hadn't forgiven him for wanting to send the boys home early. Who knew what the reasons were.

He headed into the shower but he couldn't drown out J.D.'s words to him. He was glad for the steamed-over mirror because it meant he didn't have to see his own reflection. He yanked back the thin, unfashionable bedspread and threw himself down on the mattress.

It's never too late.

He punched the pillow into shape beneath his head and turned. But that only left him looking at the door to the connecting room.

The one that he'd expected to be open.

He finally sat up again, flipping on the ugly lamp affixed to the wall between the two beds. He picked up the phone and dialed the room number next door. Through the thin walls, he could hear it ringing. Yeah, it would wake them all up, but he was a selfish man, wasn't he?

Only Susan didn't pick up the ringing telephone. Nor did she answer when he knocked on the door. If ignoring him was her latest attempt to teach him a lesson, the only thing she was succeeding in doing was making his irritation mount. He yanked on his clothes and his coat and headed to the office, intending to get the attendant to fork over the key to Susan's room even if he had to bribe the guy.

But it all went flying out the window when the kid, who had purple hair and a nose ring, informed Jake that the party in the next room had checked out.

He stiffened like a shot. "When? Where'd they go?"

"I dunno. The old lady turned in the key and drove off in a sweet SUV this afternoon. You're still paying for the room, right?" he added, as if the worrisome thought had just occurred.

Jake turned away and left the office, walking blindly.

She'd left. His suddenly independent aunt had taken his kids, and she'd left. She'd realized he was right—some things *were* too late—and done exactly what he'd wanted her to do.

So why the bloody hell did it feel so damn bad?

He wasn't even aware of how far he walked. Or how cold it was until a door swung open beside him, disgorging a few revelers, along with a wave of warmth.

He glanced at the sign over the doorway and without thinking, turned into the bar.

Inside, it was crowded. Jukebox music rocked through the place. A few couples were dancing on a miniscule dance floor. More than a few were crowded around the half dozen pool tables that lined one end.

He stared at the gleaming wood bar. A pretty, blond bartender smiled at him, her green gaze frankly appreciative. She slipped a cocktail napkin on the bar in front of him. "What can I get you?"

What the hell? Might as well live up the old man's legacy in all respects. "Glenfiddich."

The interest in her eyes increased, though the smile she gave him was wry. "Sorry. A little too top-shelf for Colbys." She looked over her shoulder at the shelving display backed by a smoky mirror that held a generous number of bottles. "Best I can do is Johnnie Walker Green."

He yanked off his coat and took the bar stool in front of her.

Taking that as assent, she pulled down the bottle. "Rocks?"

Jacob Sr. had never bothered with ice. "Neat."

She poured him a shot. Glanced at him and made it a double, then set it squarely in the center of the little cocktail napkin. She folded her arms and leaned against the bar, giving him a good look of her shapely assets if he'd been interested in looking.

He wasn't.

The only green-eyed blonde he had in his head was J.D.

"Thanks." He lifted the drink and tossed it back. Set it down again and waved his finger over it.

She tilted her head a little, but didn't argue as she poured another. "Haven't seen you in here before."

"No." He poured the whiskey down his throat, loathing the peaty malt as much as he loathed himself. J.D.'s sublime expression the night she'd tasted his Cristal swam in his brain. "Hit me again."

"That's some pricey stuff, handsome." Her lips rounded a

little when he pulled out his money clip and dropped several bills on the bar. "Okay. But if you've got car keys in your pocket, might as well hand them over, because you're not going to be fit to drive anywhere for a while and our sheriff is a bit particular about that sort of thing."

"I walked."

She looked even more curious but she pulled down a heavy crystal glass, eschewed the shot glass altogether and poured several fingers. "Sip," she advised before scooping up the cash and moving down the bar to fill another order.

He lifted the glass. The smell was strong. Familiar in the worst of ways.

"If you don't like it, why'd you order it?"

"Living down to the heritage," he murmured darkly. He lowered the glass to the bar and glanced at Ryan, who stood behind him, holding a beer in one hand and a pool cue in the other. "Might as well make it complete."

"Heritages are a bitch," Ryan agreed. He propped the cue against the bar and leaned over to toss his empty in a bin behind the bar.

Jake's lips shifted. "What I've seen of yours is a cakewalk." Every member he'd met of Ryan's family had been beyond decent. "If there's a drunk, womanizing, abusive bastard among the ranks, I'll be very surprised." His fingers turned the glass one way, then the other.

"Truth, justice and the American Way." Ryan's face was expressionless. "That's them."

J.D. hadn't been so truthful. But could Jake really blame her? She'd wanted to protect the baby from a father like him. Same reason he'd always pushed his sons away.

He lifted the glass again. The fine whiskey touched his tongue. The taste was more sour than ever. He swallowed, anyway. Instead of feeling the edge of alcohol, though, he felt more coldly sober than ever.

192   *A WEAVER BABY*

The bartender sashayed by again, placing an icy beer in front of Ryan as she passed. "Hear you're cleaning up at the tables."

"Trying." Ryan barely gave the woman a glance. "How's the colt?"

"Sliding downhill faster than ever." He gave the man the details. "J.D. won't see reason."

"She never has when it comes to horses. Only thing she puts ahead of them are the people she loves."

Jake tossed back the rest of his drink. It burned all the way down and still left him cold. "I gave Lat a chance. Not even J.D. could get him through. But she'd rather pretend he's got some sort of future left to him than face reality. She's not going to forgive me when I do what has to be done."

But Ryan shook his head. "J.D.'s no fool. If putting Latitude down ends up being the only answer left, she'll be the first one to tell you."

"She's naive. Too softhearted for her own good."

Ryan snorted. "You talking about her and that horse, or her and you?"

"No difference. Prospects are the same either way. Dead." Jake tossed another bill on the bar as he pushed off the stool. "Beer's on me." He turned away.

"Jake." Ryan stopped him with the pool cue across his chest. "I've seen the way you are together. You keep thinking the way you are, and regret's gonna become your best friend."

Jake eyed the cue. "You delivering it with that?"

Ryan's smile was grim. "Nobody'll have to lift a finger, 'cause that kind of regret comes from inside." He tapped the end of the cue against Jake's chest. "It's a helluva lot more painful."

"Not as painful as knowing I'll drive her away in the end, too." The booze was working its black magic, after all, loosening his lips in a way he didn't like at all. He headed toward the door, never more anxious to escape.

Only Ryan's pool cue barred the way again. "Obviously,

you don't know J.D. as well as you think you do. She doesn't let anyone push her anywhere. If she goes, it's because she wants to go."

"And she will," Jake said flatly. "Just like my mother when I was a kid. Hell, just like my aunt did today with my sons." He yanked the cue out of Ryan's hand.

Ryan just replaced the cue with his body. "Your aunt and sons are at J.D.'s parents' place." In less than a blink, the cue was in his hand again and Jake wasn't even sure how it had gotten there.

"You boys all right?" The blond bartender appeared beside them, settling her hands on their shoulders. "I don't need any trouble in here."

Jake shook her off, eyeing Ryan. "How do you know?"

"Because Dan mentioned it when I called to let him know I'd taken care of the horses at J.D.'s place." Ryan didn't back down. "I don't know what's gone on in your past, but around here it looks to me like you're the only one doing any running out."

Jake stepped around Ryan and headed for the exit. The air slapped him hard in the face when he reached the sidewalk. Somehow, Ryan managed to beat him there. "Now where are you going?"

"To Dan and Maggie's."

The other man let out a bark of laughter that sent vapors clouding around their heads. "You ain't gonna get there on foot, man."

Jake grimaced. "I know that." He stepped off the curb and nearly landed on his face.

"Come on, Cinderella," Ryan muttered, pulling Jake up. "How many shots did you have?"

"Just about six." The bartender had followed them out. She held out Jake's coat. "Think he might be wanting this."

Jake straightened up and pulled on his coat. He turned in

the direction of the motel. "You're starting to irritate me," he told Ryan, who silently kept pace.

"And you're not in any shape to drive." He gestured toward a pickup parked slantwise into the curb. "Get in."

He got in and Ryan headed out of town, only stopping long enough to buy two cups of coffee from a convenience store along the way. "It's the middle of the night. You want to show up there stinking drunk?"

If he'd felt stinking drunk, he might have felt better. He drank the coffee, anyway.

Daniel and Maggie Clay's house was dark when they arrived, but Ryan didn't seem to have any trouble finding his way around as they moved quietly through the rooms to the downstairs. "My cousins and I pretty much grew up in each other's houses," he told him softly as he flipped on a small lamp. "Boys are in there," he gestured to one darkened doorway. "Susan's across the hall."

Jake stared into the shadows. He wasn't even aware of Ryan silently disappearing again.

It's never too late.

J.D. had told him that. Susan had told him that.

He followed the gleam of yellow light through the doorway. The sight of the untidy humps in the two beds there nearly undid him.

He hadn't wanted to let himself believe it. But they really *were* there.

They hadn't left.

It wasn't too late.

He moved to the side of the closest bed. Pulled the quilt back across Connor's splayed limbs. His son mumbled something into his pillow and shoved his leg right back out from beneath the bedding.

Same thing he'd done when he was a baby.

Zach on the other hand was flat on his back, pillows tumbling half off the bed, his arms tossed over his head, snoring softly.

Jake picked up the pillow, his fingers digging into it. His eyes burned and he sank down onto the foot of Zach's bed. The snoring halted and he was abruptly staring into his son's eyes. "Mom's dead," Zach said flatly.

"God, no." Jake tossed the pillow on to the bed. "No, Zach. Your mom is fine."

Zach didn't budge. "Then what're you doing here?"

He ran his hands down his face. He could still taste the whiskey on his tongue, mingled with the worst coffee he'd ever drunk. He looked at his son. "I'm sorry about Adam." His voice was raw. "I know you loved him. That you miss him."

Zach sat up, pulling his knees up beneath the blankets. Drawing his feet farther away from where Jake sat. "So?" He looked across at Connor, but his brother still slept.

"So, I wanted you to know that." His jaw ached. "And to know that I—" God. Getting the words out shouldn't be so hard. "That I love you."

Zach, though, wasn't going to be that easy of a sell. He crossed his arms over his chest and glared a little harder, obviously unimpressed. *"So?"*

Running Forco and its several thousand employees was easier than facing down a rightfully suspicious nine-year-old. "So, I know I'm not much of a replacement for Adam, but I'm gonna try."

"Yeah, right," Zach muttered. "By paying the tuition at places like Penley."

"By not sending you to any more places where you don't want to go. Like Penley." He unclenched his fists. "By trying to be the kind of father you've always deserved. I know I've got a lot of years to make up for. I'm just saying that I'm going to try. And I—" He let out a breath. "I'm asking you to give me a chance. A chance to…do better."

In the other bed, Connor stirred. He leaned up on his arms, eyeing them both. "What's wrong?"

"Jake thinks he gets to have a do-over and act like a dad."

Connor's head dropped back to his pillow. "He is a dad," he said sleepily. "He just never wanted to be."

The words were like arrows. "I always wanted to be," he corrected gruffly. "But I was afraid I'd screw up as badly as my father did."

Connor's head lifted. "What'd *he* do?"

"He drank and he made sure I knew he never loved me."

Zach gave an exaggerated sniff. "And you're different? You smell like the stuff Grandpa Bill has on New Year's Eve."

"I am different." His hands fisted. "I will be different."

Zach leaned forward, his narrow, gangly body tense. "Why do you care all of a sudden?"

"I've always cared. I love you. Both of you." *It's never too late*.

"It's 'cause of J.D." Connor plopped his head into his pillow again. "'Cause he's in love with her."

Jake jerked, staring at him. "What makes you say that?"

"Duh." Zach rolled his eyes and gave him a pitying look. "Mom always says you're the smartest man she ever knew. Like in business and stuff? But you are *really* dumb."

He was surprised that his ex-wife had anything positive to say about him. "Then you're gonna have to help me out some."

"I like J.D.," Connor offered. "When she has her baby, maybe he can come visit us in California."

"Maybe you guys could stay here."

"There's no boarding school in Weaver," Zach scoffed. "And *you* don't live here, either."

"There's public school. And what if I were thinking about living here?"

"You're not gonna take us away from Mom."

"I'm not trying to," he said. "But it's going to be a long

while, yet, before she's home and can take care of you. You could stay here. And I'll bring her out to visit you when she can travel."

"You would?" Connor looked at him with pure shock.

"If that's what it takes." He could tolerate his ex-wife if it meant keeping the boys near. If it meant proving to J.D. that he could be the man she believed him to be. "So, are you gonna let me try?" He eyed them both. "I don't expect to make things perfect overnight. I don't expect to make things perfect, ever. I didn't learn how to be a father from my father." He squeezed the pillow tighter. "So, I'm going to have to learn from my sons."

Connor and Zach looked at each other. Looked back at Jake. "I'm not calling you *Dad*," Zach said after a minute.

"I don't care what you call me." He stood up between the two beds. "But make no mistake. I *am* your dad. If you pull another stunt like you did in the lab at Penley," he looked into Connor's face, "or do anything else stupid like jumping off the roof of the barn," he looked into Zach's, "you're gonna pay the price. But you're never going to have to wonder whether I love you. Got it?"

Zach slowly pulled the pillow out of Jake's fist. "Yeah. Just don't kill the pillow."

He shoved the thing under his head and slid down into bed once again.

Connor lay down too, kicking his covers a little more. "Are y'gonna marry J.D.?"

The boys hadn't pulled their punches with him so far, so Jake didn't know why the question hit him so hard. "I wasn't that good at marriage." Until J.D., he'd never thought he'd have reason to care about it again.

"You weren't that good at being a dad," Zach pointed out, ever blunt. "But you're trying that again, aren't you?"

Chapter Seventeen

Jake wasn't at the clinic when J.D. arrived there the next morning. But since she'd seen his fancy truck parked outside the Sleep Tite—sticking out like a sore thumb among the motley collection of other vehicles there—she wasn't surprised.

What she *was,* was numb.

Numb in a way that had nothing to do with a pain pill.

She found Evan inside his clinic with Latitude.

The colt was lying down again and she slipped into the stall with him. His ears barely pricked with interest.

"How was his night?" She looked up at Evan but felt a little more hope drain away at his expression.

"I had to increase the pain drip to keep him comfortable."

"Has Dr. Windsor been by, yet?"

"He and Jake left about an hour ago."

She hadn't expected them to meet so early. Her heart sank as surely as she did, sitting in the sand alongside the horse. "I don't want to know what they said, do I." It wasn't a question.

"Probably not. You already know, anyway."

She bit her lip. "What do *you* think?"

Evan crouched down beside her, running his long fingers over Latitude's long neck. "I think Latitude has a hellacious battle on his hands."

"One he can't win?"

"I didn't say that."

"You agree with Windsor, then?"

"I didn't say that, either."

"Well what *do* you say, Evan?" Her voice rose a little but he just eyed her back with kind patience and she let out a sigh. "I'm sorry."

"Times like this when we all wish we had a crystal ball. We don't. You know what Latitude is facing. The bone's just the start of his problems. If it continues to heal, if the laminitis is successfully treated, if it doesn't recur—or spread. He'll never race to compete, but it's conceivable that Lat could have a good, decent life. Getting him to that point, however, putting him through it—" He shook his head slightly and pushed himself to his feet.

"Letting go is sometimes the kinder act," she whispered, struggling against the pressure building behind her eyes. "You're going to handle it, then." Who more qualified to end a horse's life than a man trained to save it?

"I told Jake yesterday that I would if it came to this."

She looked away. Stared blindly into the corners of the stall. "I'm going to stay with him."

"Jake's not going to allow that, J.D. Not when he knows how upset you are."

"Some things Jake doesn't get to decide." She dragged a bag of peppermints out of her pocket and unwrapped one. "I'm staying."

But unlike every other time she'd offered Latitude a mint, he didn't take it.

He just slid his beautifully formed head over her knee, huffed a little, and closed his eyes.

She bowed her head, stroking her hand down his neck. Tears dripped down her face. Wiping them away only made room for more.

Evan left. Her parents arrived. Her brother. A parade of family. Every one of them tried to convince her to leave Latitude's stall only to back down, like Evan, in the face of her resolve.

When she heard yet another set of footsteps stop outside of the stall, she didn't even look up. "I'm not leaving."

"Ever?"

Her head snapped up at Jake's gruff voice. She looked up at him.

He wore jeans and a black sweater. His eyes were blood-shot and his face was lined.

He looked as haggard as she felt and she ached even more inside.

She wouldn't make the mistake again of thinking he'd come to this decision easily.

She curled her fingers into Latitude's mane. The horse was awake, his liquid eyes shifting from her to Jake and back again. "I don't agree with what you're planning." Her throat felt raw. "And I know that it's your decision to make. But I'm going to stay with him to the end."

He stepped into the stall, scattering a few peppermints when his boot knocked into the bag. Latitude's prone position didn't leave much room. He crouched down and picked up one of the plastic-wrapped candies. "Is Lat the only one you'd never give up on?"

The question came out of left field and the ache inside her grew even more acute. "I don't give up on anything I love," she said carefully.

He was silent for a long moment, seeming to stare at the candy in his hand. "What about *anyone?*"

Her heart jerked. "Or…any…*one*."

"Even me?"

Her lips parted. She couldn't have said a word to save her soul.

He shifted and pulled an envelope out of his pocket. "Here." He lifted it slightly when she just stared at it. "Take it."

She swallowed and slowly slid the envelope out of his grasp. The envelope was plain white, except for a return address and logo for the Sleep Tite in the corner. And there was only one thin sheet inside when she looked. "What is it?"

"Proof of ownership. I've signed Latitude over to you."

"What?"

His jaw canted slightly. "Money won't be an issue." His tone was ragged. "You can make whatever decisions you want about him. Treatment. Surgery. Whatever rehabilitation he needs. I'll pay it all. And if the—*when* the day comes, you can turn him out to chase all the damn butterflies you want."

The envelope slid out of her nerveless fingers. It fluttered to the sand beneath her knees. Latitude brushed his nose against it. Briefly curious. Just as quickly losing interest. "You're serious."

"I told Windsor when I saw him earlier. He doesn't think it's likely to change the end results, but he's agreed to come back if Lat needs more surgery."

She could hardly breathe. "Why are you doing this?"

He looked at Latitude.

Ran his hand slowly down his sleek, powerful body.

"Because you love this horse." His voice was low. Gruff. "And I love you."

Her heart climbed right into her throat. The words were so perfect to her ears. And so impossibly unexpected. "No." She shook her head. "You don't let yourself love anyone."

"That's true." He looked at her. "Until I shared a glass of Cristal with you one hot summer night, and everything started to change." His gaze dropped to her belly. "I just didn't know how much until I came here."

She swallowed. Her pulse was thundering inside her. "I wish I'd told you from the first."

"I think this is where we'd still have ended." His voice was hushed. "I want to believe it is."

Her nerves squeezed. "Ended?"

"Ended up," he amended. His gaze ran over her face. "I talked to the boys last night after I took you home. Yeah." He grimaced when her eyebrows rose. "It was pretty damn late. And I was heading toward being pretty damn drunk."

"No."

"Ask Ryan someday. He'll tell you." He moved his hand over Latitude's back again. His fingers stopped inches shy of hers. "I don't want to be my father," he said abruptly. "I don't want my kids—any of them—pushing away the people that matter because they're too afraid of getting hurt. I want them to be the kind of person who can look at a lost cause and still believe that it's not...too...late."

His deep voice cracked and her heart seemed to crack open right along with it.

She moved her fingers those few inches until they grazed his. "You're not a lost cause."

His eyes searched hers. "Are you sure?"

She looked from the envelope and back to him. "I would be certain of it, even if you hadn't done this. Made this...in-credible...gift." A gift that would leave her reeling for some time. "But if this is about the baby—*our* baby—you don't have to worry. I'll never make the mistake again of thinking he's better off without a father. Without you."

He turned his hand and slid his fingers through hers. "You said you loved me. Did you mean it?"

She was simply incapable of holding anything back. "Yes."

"Is that just because of the baby?"

Her brows drew together. She shook her head. "No." Her admission dropped like a pebble in the silence. "I love you even more because of the baby."

His fingers tightened around hers. "Then can't I feel the same way?" He leaned closer. His eyes burned fiercely. "I never expected you in my life, J.D. Clay. Not like this. I never expected another chance to be a better man. But now I've got it and I'm scared to death of blowing it. And I'm giving you Latitude because he's the one thing I have that I know matters to you."

"Oh, Jake." She let out a broken laugh. Her heart wasn't in her throat anymore. It was in her chest, and just about ready to explode. "You still don't get it, do you?"

His eyes darkened. His body tensed.

She slid her arm out of the sling and leaned closer to him. "There's something you can give me that I value even more than Latitude." She settled her palm against his chest. *"Your heart."*

His jaw twisted. He closed his hand over hers, pressing it hard against the beat that she could plainly feel. "The horse is a better bet." His voice was harsh.

But she heard the uncertainty lurking there, anyway.

She could show endless patience with a skittish horse.

How could she give Jake anything less than a lifetime, if that's how long it took?

She slowly leaned over Latitude until her lips were only a breath from his. Her eyes stared into his. "I was never much of a gambler," she whispered. "I only bet on sure things."

His hands slid to her face. They were shaking. "And *are* you sure? It's not like you're getting a bargain, J.D. My family's barely functioning. I have responsibilities at Forco. There're going to be times when I can't be here in Weaver. Times when I know I'm going to mess up. I swear to you, I'll try not to, but marriage to me—"

"Marriage!" She straightened like a shot, staring at him with fresh shock.

"What'd you think I was talking about?"

She blinked. "I didn't know you wanted to *marry* me!" Just like that, she was the one shaking.

Jake slowly drew her back to him. "Then let's be clear." He gently nudged her chin up until her eyes met his. "I love you, J. D. Clay. I'm not sure I even had a heart, until you came along. But you did, and it's yours. So will you forget all good sense and logic that should tell you to choose otherwise, and agree to be my wife?"

"My good sense and logic are smart enough to listen to my heart," she returned tartly, only to ruin it with the tears that crept down her face.

This time, though, the tears had nothing to do with grief.

And everything to do with hope.

His thumb slid slowly over her cheeks, drawing up the moisture, and the tenderness there would have undone her resistance if he hadn't already succeeded in dissolving it to bits. "And what's your heart saying?"

She pulled in a shaking breath. Let it out in an even longer one. "It's saying *yes*."

Jake didn't move. Only the gleam of his dark brown eyes ranged over her face, as if he wanted to memorize the moment.

"Yes, Jake," she whispered again. "Yes. I will be your wife."

It seemed forever in coming. But the smile that hinted around his lips finally took hold. It widened. It spread. Until it slowly slid to his eyes and pushed aside the shadows that were there.

Then he let out a bark of laughter and pressed his mouth to hers.

Neither one particularly noticed when Latitude huffed and pushed out of their way, shuffling ungainly to his feet. Or when he stuck his head down and nosed around into the bag of peppermints....

Epilogue

May

"Happy Birthday, Mommy." Jake leaned over J.D. and the blanket-draped infant she held to her shoulder, and pressed a kiss to both of their heads.

J.D. leaned against the wooden rail fencing beside her and looked up at him. Beyond them, acres of rolling fields were only a shade lighter than her dancing emerald eyes. "It's not my birthday. Nor is it Tuck's."

Tucker Reeves Forrest. Jake peeled the blanket farther away and grazed his third son's velvety cheek with the edge of his finger. Tuck had come almost eight weeks early, giving them all a healthy scare and derailing their original wedding date. But their son had his mother's emerald eyes and both his and J.D.'s determination.

And now, exactly two months since his birth, he was as

strong and feisty as they could have prayed. "It's his two-month birthday," Jake said. "Let me celebrate."

J.D.'s laughter was soft. The breeze tugged her hair, scattering a few white blossoms from the curling mass where they'd been pinned. "You don't have enough to celebrate today?" She leaned up and kissed his lips, taking a gentle nip along the way. "You're the one who chose Derby day when we had to reschedule our wedding," she reminded.

It was the first Saturday in May and for the first time in more years than he could remember, he had no horses running in the Kentucky Derby. Not even Platinum Cross, who'd been one of the favorites coming into the season.

Right now, Latitude was in the field behind them, tearing around like he was on fire with Ziggy hard on his heels when he wasn't stopping next to J.D. to drag at the flowers in her hair.

"And I'll never be able to forget I've won a prize worth more than any race," he told her. Which is exactly why he'd chosen Derby day. And why Forrest's Crossing was *not* running any horses there this year.

Her eyes went soft and mossy. She rested her palm along his jaw. "I love you, Mr. Forrest."

"And I love you, Mrs. Forrest."

"Enough kissing already," Maggie came over to them and lifted Tuck out of J.D.'s arms. "Susan's been trying to catch your attention for the last half hour!" She kissed his son's tiny nose. "Squire's getting impatient for that cake to be cut so he can get on with his fishing trip with your best men and I swear, I wouldn't put it past the old coot to start cutting it himself." She gestured toward the barn, where guests milled around the laden tables. "Move it!"

"Are you going to be like your mother when you're her age?" Jake asked, watching Maggie stride away, the folds of her airy yellow dress floating behind her, along with the trailing edge of Tuck's blanket.

J.D. ducked again from Latitude's affectionate nudges and leaned across the fence, swatting him on the rump. "Go play." The horse lifted his head and blew out a noisy breath. Then he spotted Ziggy and launched himself after him running with an ease and an enthusiasm that proved all of J.D.'s faith had been well placed.

His wife's smile was more brilliant than ever as she turned back to Jake and tucked her hand through his arm. The wedding ring he'd placed on her finger only a few hours earlier winked in the sunlight. "We can only hope I'm like my mother." She shot him a teasing look. "My parents are still hot for each other."

He laughed and they made their way toward the rest of the reception. "I'll give you hot."

She slanted him a look. "I know," she said, dulcet.

It was a mistake for him to ever think he'd have an edge on this woman.

It had been five months since he'd started his life, thanks to her. Five months of arranging schedules, of them both shuttling back and forth to Forrest's Crossing while he realigned things at Forco so Charlotte could assume more responsibilities, and J.D. supervised the plans to bring Crossing West into fruition on the Hanks spread that they'd closed on after Christmas. Between the kids and Latitude's rocky recovery—three more surgeries and a half dozen casts—along with everything else, it seemed there'd hardly been time to breathe.

But J.D. had made sure he remembered there was always time to love.

They reached the linen-draped table that sat in the shadow of the deep red barn that Ryan had finished painting well before the snow started to melt off. All around them, J.D.'s place—*their* place—was decorated with white flowers. They swayed in the breeze where they draped over the corrals, hung in bunches from the opened barn doors, and twined around the house's porch. The sky was a perfect crystal-blue. But the real perfection didn't come from the agreeable weather, or the setting that J.D. and her family had created.

It came in the crowd joining them. In the shrieking giggles as kids raced back and forth. In the hugs and the laughter and the talk.

Loving J.D. hadn't just gotten him Tucker. Or his sons. He'd found himself in the middle of more family, more friends, than he'd ever dreamed possible.

He was pretty sure that every member of the Clay family was present and accounted for. And even though J.D. had warned him just how many there were, it was still a startling sight to see.

Then J.D.'s hand slid into his and she tugged him to the side of the towering wedding cake, sized to satisfy the sweet tooth of everyone there.

"Where are the best men?" Susan looked vaguely frazzled. "Jake, you said you'd keep an eye on them!"

"And I have," he assured. He went to the barn and yelled inside. "Zach. Con. Get out here and get your pictures taken."

A moment later, his sons trotted out. Their gray suit jackets were gone, their white shirts smudged with dirt. They looked pretty much like they'd been rolling around in the barn, and maybe they had been.

That day, Jake wasn't going to care and he knew that J.D. wouldn't, either. His aunt, though, just tsked when she saw them. She swiped her hands down Zach's shoulders and pushed back Connor's tumbled hair then shooed them toward Jake and J.D. "What are we going to do with you two?"

With a grin, Connor just shrugged and followed Zach around the table. "Dunno," Zach said. He licked the finger that he'd slyly swiped through a curl of white icing. "What're you gonna do with us, Jake?" They were already grounded for two weeks, thanks to a science experiment that had gotten out of hand. They only had another few weeks of school left, and then they would be heading to San Francisco for a month with Tiffany.

The accident she'd narrowly survived had left her forever changed. When he and J.D. had approached her to share the boys' time, she'd actually agreed that it was a good thing.

He glanced at Zach. "I can tell you that fishing with Squire this weekend is off." But he grinned before Zach's expression fell too far. Both he and Connor had found a buddy who was just as wily as they were. The fact that he happened to be J.D.'s aging grandfather was immaterial to all of them.

Susan had her camera in hand again, and was gesturing for them to move closer together. Jake took Tucker and propped him against his shoulder, facing the camera.

"Now that is a beautiful family." Susan lifted her camera.

"Wait." Jake gestured to Brody, the sardonic lawyer who was standing next to his very pregnant wife. "Take the camera, will you? She should be in this picture, too."

Brody strolled over and lifted the camera from Susan's hands. "You heard the man."

She dashed her hands down her dress and moved over, joining them. Jake handed Tuck to her. "There you go, auntie."

Susan's eyes were a little damp. She rubbed her cheek against the tuft of blond hair on Tuck's otherwise bald head.

"Smile into the camera," Jake advised, and wrapped his arms around J.D.

And smile, they did.

*Mills & Boon® Special Moments™
brings you a sneak preview…*

*Turn the page for a peek at this fantastic new
story from Victoria Pade, available next
month in Mills & Boon!*

*When Tate McCord caught reporter Tanya Kimbrough
snooping around the McCord mansion for business
secrets, he had to admit – the housekeeper's daughter
had become a knockout! The real scoop – this Texas
Cinderella was about to steal the surgeon's heart.*

she'd thought she would be in and out long before any of the McCords got home…

Make a run for it the way you came in, she advised herself.

She certainly couldn't turn off the library lights without drawing attention since the doors to the living room were ajar. But maybe Tate and Blake McCord would only think someone had forgotten to turn them off before they'd left the house tonight. And if she went out the way she'd come in, no one would guess that she'd used her mother's keys to let herself in through the French doors that opened to the rear grounds of the sprawling estate. If she just left right now…

But then Blake McCord answered his brother and she stayed where she was. What she was listening to suited her purposes so much better than what she'd already found on the library desk.

"Finding the Santa Magdalena and buying up canary diamonds for a related jewelry line are in the works," Blake was saying. "And we've launched the initial Once In A Lifetime promotional campaign in the stores to pamper customers and bring in more business. That's all you have to know since you—and everyone else—are on a need-to-know-only basis. Your time and interest might be better spent paying some attention to your fiancée, wouldn't you say?"

"What I'd say is that *that* isn't any of your business," Tate answered in a tone that surprised Tanya.

The sharp edge coming from Tate didn't sound anything like him. The brothers generally got along well, and Tate had always been the easygoing brother. Tanya's mother had said that Tate had changed since spending a year working in the Middle East and suddenly Tanya didn't doubt it.

"It may not be my business, but I'm telling you anyway because someone has to," Blake persisted. "You take Katie for granted, you neglect her, you don't pay her nearly enough attention. You may think you have her all sewed up with that engagement ring on her finger, but if you don't start giving her some indication that you know she's alive, she could end up throwing it in your face. And nobody would blame her if she did."

Katie was Katerina Whitcomb-Salgar, the daughter of the McCord family's longtime friends and the woman everyone had always assumed would end up as Mrs. Tate McCord long before their formal engagement was announced.

"You're going to lose Katie," Blake shouted, some heat in his voice now. "And if you do, it'll serve you right."

"Or it might be for the best," Tate countered, enough under his breath that Tanya barely made out what he'd said. Then more loudly again, he added, "Just keep your eye on finding that diamond and getting McCord's Jewelers and the family coffers healthy again. Since you want to carry all the weight for that yourself, you shouldn't have a lot of spare time to worry about my love life, too. But if I want your advice, I'll be sure to ask for it."

"You need someone's advice or you're going to blow the best thing that ever happened to you."

"Thanks for the heads-up," Tate said facetiously.

And then there were footsteps.

But only some of them moved away from the library.

The others were coming closer…

Too late to run.

Tanya ducked for cover, hoping that since she was behind the desk whoever was headed her way wouldn't be able to see her when he reached in and turned off the lights.

"Tate hasn't even been staying in the house since he got back. He's living in the guest cottage…"

Tanya's mother's words flashed through her mind just then and it struck her that merely having the lights turned off might not be what was about to happen. That Tate might use the library route to go to the guesthouse that was also out back....

Tanya's heart had begun to race the minute she'd heard the McCords' voices. Now it was pounding. Because while she might have been able to explain her presence in the library at this time of night, how would she ever explain crouching behind the desk?

Or holding the papers she'd been looking through— because until that minute she hadn't even realized she'd taken them with her when she'd ducked.

Please don't come in here....

"What the hell?"

Oh, no...

Tanya had tried to turn herself into a small ball but when Tate McCord's voice boomed from nearby, she raised her head to find him leaning over the front of the desk, clearly able to see her.

This was much, much worse than when she was six and had been caught with her fingers in the icing of his twin sisters' birthday cake. His mother Eleanor had been kind and understanding. But there was nothing kind or understanding in Tate McCord's face at that moment.

Summoning what little dignity she could—and with the papers still in hand—Tanya stood.

It was the first time she and Tate McCord had set eyes on each other in the seven years since Tanya had left for college. And even before that—when Tate had come home from his own university and medical school training for vacations or visits while Tanya still lived on the property with her mother—there weren't many occasions when the McCord heir had crossed paths with the housekeeper's daughter. Plus, Tanya had been very well aware of the fact that, more often than not, when any of the McCords had seen her, they'd looked through her rather than at her.

So she wasn't sure Tate McCord recognized her and, as if it would make this better, she said, "You probably don't remember me—"

"You're JoBeth's daughter—Tanya," he said bluntly. "What the hell are you doing in here at this hour and—"

He glanced down at the papers and held out his hand in a silent demand for her to give them to him.

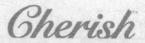
910/023b

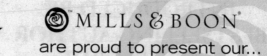

2 FREE BOOKS
AND A SURPRISE GIFT

We would like to take this opportunity to thank you for reading this Mills & Boon® book by offering you the chance to take TWO more specially selected books from the Special Moments™ series absolutely FREE! We're also making this offer to introduce you to the benefits of the Mills & Boon® Book Club™—

- **FREE home delivery**
- **FREE gifts and competitions**
- **FREE monthly Newsletter**
- **Exclusive Mills & Boon Book Club offers**
- **Books available before they're in the shops**

Accepting these FREE books and gift places you under no obligation to buy, you may cancel at any time, even after receiving your free books. Simply complete your details below and return the entire page to the address below. You don't even need a stamp!

YES Please send me 2 free Special Moments books and a surprise gift. I understand that unless you hear from me, I will receive 5 superb new stories every month, including a 2-in-1 book priced at £4.99 and three single books priced at £3.19 each, postage and packing free. I am under no obligation to purchase any books and may cancel my subscription at any time. The free books and gift will be mine to keep in any case.

Ms/Mrs/Miss/Mr _____ Initials _____

Surname _____

Address _____

_____

_____ Postcode _____

E-mail _____

Send this whole page to: Mills & Boon Book Club, Free Book Offer, FREEPOST NAT 10298, Richmond, TW9 1BR

Offer valid in UK only and is not available to current Mills & Boon Book Club subscribers to this series. Overseas and Eire please write for details.. We reserve the right to refuse an application and applicants must be aged 18 years or over. Only one application per household. Terms and prices subject to change without notice. Offer expires 30th November 2010. As a result of this application, you may receive offers from Harlequin Mills & Boon and other carefully selected companies. If you would prefer not to share in this opportunity please write to The Data Manager, PO Box 676, Richmond, TW9 1WU.

Mills & Boon® is a registered trademark owned by Harlequin Mills & Boon Limited.
Special Moments™ is being used as a trademark.
The Mills & Boon® Book Club™ is being used as a trademark.